LOUISE'S SECRET

LIA GOODACRE

Louise's Secret

Lia Goodacre

1

L ondon 1855

The moment Louise Thomas stepped into the lecture hall, the hum of conversation hushed almost to silence. Anyone would have thought it was this elegant young woman who was giving the lecture. But it was her reputation amongst engineering circles that was the real reason. Ignoring the whispers that followed, she descended the steps of the auditorium at the Institution of Civil Engineers to find a seat in the audience.

Her pretty nose wrinkled when she noticed the faint aroma of cigar smoke. Such a nuisance, she hated the smell, but knew she must put up with such things for the sake of experiencing the engineering world first hand. The plain white, arched ceiling matched the unpretentious functional room, just as she would have expected of a building dedicated to the work of the great men of the age.

Soon enough, her arrival was forgotten and the noise of people talking in the room increased.

"I do hope today's lecture is better than yesterday's," she said to her elderly companion, Mrs Rothers. They paused halfway down the steps until a portly gentleman made room for them on the plain wooden benches. "Yesterday we weren't given enough detail, and Mr Lodge's condescension was unbearable at times. I don't understand why they asked him to speak."

Mrs Rothers's wrinkled hand touched her friend's arm. "Louise, you must make allowances, Mr Lodge is far more used to speaking to his fellow engineers and not the general public. He probably thought we were all simpletons."

"I could forgive him that, but he spoke nothing of when his great ship would be finished, or whether he had completed a scaled model to see if the thing would actually float! The very fact that he designed it to be a paddle ship was laughable. Everyone knows that propellers are the way forward in ship design," she said, with a dismissive wave of her hand and a small laugh.

"Perhaps he didn't like the tone in which you told him that yesterday."

Louise sighed. "Maybe you're right, but I'm not sorry I questioned him. If he were a better engineer than he thinks he is, I wouldn't have issue."

Mrs Rothers glanced around the auditorium. "We'd best hope that today's engineer will be more considerate."

Louise's gaze followed her friend's across the sea of men in dark coats, only occasionally interrupted by a lady. "Yes, I'm sure he will be. Today's lecture is to be given by Charles Lucas, and I have heard much about him. They say he is the next Brunel; a rising star, soon to be elevated among the great engineers of our time."

"Really? I've heard he is very handsome." Mrs Rothers gave a knowing smile.

"Trust you to mention that! But I wouldn't know." Louise brushed a speck of dirt from her pale green muslin dress. It was one of her plainer ones, but with an intricate thin white lace shawl and straw hat, she exuded elegance. "I don't think about that sort of thing. It's intelligence that matters to me, though I have heard that he is quite passionate about his work. Which of those gentlemen do you think he is?"

She looked over to front of the auditorium and tried to quell a growing sense of anticipation. In a few moments she would set eyes on the man she had heard so much about. There were three gentlemen talking, any of which could be Mr Lucas. Each was dressed in a dark suit, with only a different-coloured cravat to distinguish them.

"Perhaps the stocky gentleman with the blonde hair?" Mrs Rothers replied.

"No! Surely not. He is far too old. Mr Lucas is, I believe, only thirty."

"You seem to know a lot about him." Mrs Rothers fanned herself with the programme.

"I know a little, but that gentleman you indicated is at least forty-five. I'll wager you five pounds he is that man seated over there." Louise pointed to a gentleman sitting on the front row. "He is clearly not a member of the audience; he is holding notes and drawings of the bridge." As Mrs Rothers was about to answer, that same man stood up, placed his notes onto the oak reading stand and waited for the audience to fall silent.

"Good afternoon," he said when the room hushed. "I'm Charles Lucas, and in today's lecture I will be talking to you about my bridge across the Tamar."

"You owe me five pounds," Louise whispered to Mrs Rothers with a mischievous grin. Much to Louise's pleasure, the lecture was a much more agreeable experience than the previous day's. Mr Lucas spoke about his suspension bridge with much enthusiasm, and Louise eagerly took notes.

Despite her previous protestations to Mrs Rothers, Louise did notice how tall Mr Lucas was, and how his dark hair suited his dark eyes.Though perhaps not particularly handsome in the conventional way, he was certainly not unpleasant to look at. He possessed a confidence that surpassed any plainness in the face. His eyes scanned his audience, gauging their reaction as he spoke. Though he was a little serious in his countenance, she supposed speaking to such a large amount of people must make him at least a little nervous. She wasn't disappointed with the man she had heard so much of. His partnership, Lucas and Ashton, was well known throughout engineering circles as one of the best, and if she was a little in awe, then it only showed in her concentration and wide eyes while she listened.

She had a myriad of questions to ask him, but she didn't dare while he spoke; her usual confidence temporarily escaped her. Strange, she wasn't usually this controlled when she was eager with queries. But she didn't want to disturb him or miss anything he said. He talked of the bridge design competition, of his inspiration, his visit to the site where the bridge would be built, and his project plan for the building schedule. She wrote it all down in her notebook, until her pencil was blunted.

When Mr Lucas finished speaking, forty-five minutes later, he asked his attentive listeners for questions. Louise's hand shot up in the air immediately. "Why do you think your design was chosen above the others submitted?" she asked in a clear voice.

"Well, obviously the judges decided it was the best design," he replied with a smile.

A small ripple of laughter went through the lecture hall.

Louise ignored the audience reaction and asked, "Did you see the other designs before they were submitted?"

"No, but I have seen them since, and I can assure you the judges chose wisely."

More laughter.

"Do you think you would have won the competition if Mr Brunel had entered it?"

The auditorium hushed in an instant. Then there were a few whispers around her. Several people in front of her turned and stared at her. She thought she heard someone mutter "Impudent". Mr Lucas was momentarily speechless. His expression grew serious and he answered in a business-like tone, "We will never know. I was a little disappointed that Mr Brunel didn't enter, but other projects take up most of his time these days. Or so I hear."

Louise glanced at her list of questions. "Is work started on the bridge?"

"Yes. Some of the preliminary work has begun."

"How many men will you need?"

"Current estimates are three hundred," he answered.

"Do you think there will be many casualties amongst your workers?"

"I hope not. So far I have an exemplary record in that regard. The safety of my workers is of paramount impor-tance to me, unlike some other engineers."

"How will you choose your contractors? Will you simply pick the cheapest?"

"Absolutely not. I will choose the best. I'm very careful to judge my contractors on their past experience and success." He gave her an earnest stare, as though adding weight to his words.

Louise felt Mrs Rothers's hand on her arm and a swift

glance at her friend told her she should keep from asking anything else.

More questions ensued from others in the audience, and Mr Lucas answered with equal attention. Louise thought they asked rather basic things and wondered how he didn't lose patience; she found his restraint admirable.

When the questions finished, Mr Lucas was awarded a round of applause and people began to leave. Mrs Rothers turned to her friend. "Did he meet with your approval?"

Louise gave a wide smile. "Of course. I only have one complaint. . ."

"Yes?"

"He didn't talk for long enough."

They both stood up and made their way to the aisle.

"I expect you will want to view the bridge design at the front?" Mrs Rothers asked.

"Do you mind?"

"Not at all. I will see you again tomorrow; take as long as you need."

Mrs Rothers started to walk away, then turned back for a brief moment, "My dear, when you speak to Mr Lucas again, try not to scare him."

It was a few minutes before Louise could find a way through the throng to look at the bridge design more closely. But eventually, she was allowed the luxury of examining the documents closely. She pulled out her notebook again, and started to sketch the bridge.

"I hope you're not planning to use my design to enter a competition on your own?" Louise heard a voice say in a deep amused tone directly behind her.

"Oh, no!" she blushed, turning around and meeting Mr Lucas's cobalt eyes for a moment, "I – er, I just wished to get the impression of the design so that I wouldn't forget."

His tone became more serious. "I think if you were to see the other entries, and know something about the terrain where the bridge must be built, you would see why they chose mine."

"It's a difficult place to build?" She knew something of the locality, it was only forty miles from her estate, but she could comprehend little of the difficulties of building a bridge.

"Not particularly, but the clay soil near the Tamar makes many standard designs unsuitable."

She inclined her head. "Very interesting. And that is why yours was chosen above the others?"

"It was one of the main reasons, yes. But there were other aspects the panel liked too. It will hold a substantially larger amount of weight because of the height of the rungs and the specific type of steel." He added with a gleam in his eye, "And I think they liked the shape of the towers."

She gave a small laugh, then checked herself. She sounded like a flirtatious school girl. "I read your article in the Engineering Journal," she said in a more serious tone. "The one about the railway tunnel under the Pennines. Do you think it will ever be done? I heard there is still much opposition from the locals."

"You read the Engineering Journal?" A smile played on his lips and she noticed what a difference it made to his face.

"Oh yes," she said. "I don't understand all of it, but I try my best. I wish sometimes that there was another journal, or a dictionary that explained the more complicated aspects of engineering, but then I suppose it's not written for people like me. I only seem to get the general idea of things most of the time."

He nodded, not offering any other response. "Are you

going to publish an article on your bridge design?" she asked, after an awkward pause.

"I haven't thought of it, but now that you mention it, I probably will."

"Then I'll look forward to reading it."

"I will make sure the bridge design is also printed." Then he added, "So that you will not forget it and rely on your own sketches." He twisted his head to look at her sketch.

"I apologise for my appalling artwork." She blushed a little. "I have never been talented in the arts, and I have failed to do your design any justice."

"It's no matter. I spent many hours drawing and perfecting my design, I wouldn't expect anyone to be able to copy it so quickly." He leaned towards her and said quietly, "If the truth be known, I'm not a great artist either."

She was grateful for his admission but simply smiled in return.

"Did you attend the lecture yesterday?" she asked.

"No, I had a prior appointment."

Louise was about to comment on how awful she had found the lecture when they were interrupted.

"Ah, Louise, I thought you'd be here. I knew you couldn't resist a chance to hear Charles Lucas talk about his bridge."

They both turned around to see a tall blond gentleman approaching. "Lord Philip!" she exclaimed. "I wondered when I would get to see you."

They greeted each other with an affectionate kiss on the cheek. Mr Lucas retreated.

"I think you've frightened him off with all your questions," Lord Philip whispered and looked over to the other side of the room where Mr Lucas now stood.

"I'm sure I don't know what you mean." Louise

commented. She watched Mr Lucas talking to a gentleman she concluded was probably his partner, Mr Ashton.

She sighed. "I had more questions for him too, and now he is gone! He didn't answer my questions about the tunnel either." She shook her head. "Ah well, it seems I have lost my chance, but I do hope it wasn't out of offence at my queries. I would do anything rather than displease a man such as he. He is quite famous, you know."

Philip offered his arm, and she took it. He led her to the door and before she left she took one last look at Mr Lucas.

"Robert Adams chose well to invest in his work," she said.

"Indeed," Philip replied and followed her gaze. "Robert Adams always chooses his investments carefully."

The pair left the Institute and decided to walk about St James's Park to enjoy the last of the warm September sunshine. They made their way out to the more pleasing grass. Avoiding the pathways, they headed to where the ground was littered with the first fallen leaves, a hint of the autumn to come. A cool breeze rustled the brown and green of the landscaped trees. Louise looked around the park. London was so much more pleasant when the sun shined, and only half so oppressive.

"Why did you not come and see me sooner?" she asked in a playful tone. "I've been in London nearly four days." She studied his face for a moment. His brown eyes had lines underneath them, but otherwise his features were not altered from the last time she had seen him.

Lord Philip gave a dismissive laugh. "Well, you know me, I've been busy, my dear cousin."

"Doing what exactly?" she asked, looking at him with shrewd eyes.

He replied with a shrug and she knew he wouldn't

answer even if she pressed the issue. Perhaps it was better not to know. Over the years she had heard many stories about her cousin's escapades; several of which involved widowed ladies of dubious reputation. But he was always the perfect gentleman to her and as one of her few blood relatives, she valued his advice and steadfast character. If she ever needed help, she knew he would do everything he could to assist.

"Our friendship is very one-sided, Philip," she commented after a few minutes.

"My dear, you know it's best that we don't spend too much time together, otherwise people will start to talk," he said in a dry tone.

"They do enough of that about you already without any encouragement. However much we say that we will never marry, someone is always saying we might or should. This strange notion that first cousins should wed has always been odd to me."

"I suppose some like to keep their wealth in the family whatever the cost, but to me it's a peculiar idea." He led her past the lake and they stopped for a moment and watched the swans.

"Sometimes I have the impression your mother would have us marry," Louise said.

"She has mentioned it to me on more than one occasion, though I feel it was more a means to protect you than anything else. She first mentioned it when your father died."

"Really? She means well, but you do a good job of protecting me without being my husband. I've always had this strange notion that you would continue to watch over me even if I were to marry."

Philip gave a small incline of his head, indicating she was speaking the truth.

"How is my aunt?" she asked.

"She is in Edinburgh and in excellent health. She must be enjoying herself because I've heard little from her."

"She certainly does know how to take pleasure in life."

"And why not? She taught me well, after all."

"Now I realise why my father didn't like me to spend too much time with her."

Philip grinned and his eyes gleamed. "So what are the London gossips saying of me this year?"

"I'm not sure you'd like to know!" Her voice was playful. He prompted her to continue.

"Well, rumour has it that last week you danced twice with Miss Vine in the same evening, and now she expects your proposal at any moment."

"Ha! Is that all! Miss Vine? Which one was she?" He stopped walking for a moment, turned to Louise and looked into the distance. "Oh yes, the pretty blonde one, just out, and desperate to impress. She thinks she can catch me, but she's wrong. She simpers and tries to get my attention like so many women. I find it all quite tiresome. If only they would realise I relish a challenge; they would improve their chances ten-fold."

"Well I would only dance with Miss Vine once next time, if you do see her again," Louise said with a note of seriousness.

"What? Are you jealous that I've never asked you to dance twice in the same evening?"

"You know I'd always refuse if you did."

Philip gave a deep laugh. "Dear Louise, you do amuse me."

They walked on. Louise was determined to try to keep Philip to herself at least for a short time.

"How is Glazebrook?" Philip asked. "I have been

meaning to visit your estate again. It's been nearly a year since I've been there."

"Everything is well. There will be a bumper harvest this year. I'm looking forward to returning."

"You always look forward to going back. I wonder why you come to London at all."

"It's true I prefer to live in Devon, but how could I resist these lectures? I have been looking forward to them for months."

"How have you found them?"

"Today's was excellent. Yesterday's, however, was dreadful."

After fifteen minutes of explanation of both lectures, Philip declared,"Enough of your engineering talk! I do not think I can stand any more. Please speak about something else."

"Very well," Louise laughed. "I will not mention engineering again, although you know how interesting I find such things."

"Indeed, how can I forget the time when you were twelve and built your own bridge across the small stream at the bottom field at Glazebrook."

"It was an excellent bridge, if not somewhat flimsy. I spent days constructing it. Well, the servants had to move the logs for me, but I added the handrail." Louise grinned as she remembered it. It was a terrible construct and had fallen apart as soon as a storm came, but she was very proud of it at the time.

"Yes, a fine specimen of engineering it was. As I recall it was most unstable. You should explain the design to your Mr Lucas. Doubtless he will be impressed. Tell me, do you still keep those infernal miniature steam engines? And the workroom?"

"Of course."

"I thought as much. I do believe that if you were to ever marry, you should marry an engineer. But don't expect me to come to dinner very often. Or if I do, sit me away from you both so I do not have to listen your conversations." He spoke with a note of fondness in his voice. Louise was amused at the thought of Philip seated at one end of her grand dining table at Glazebrook and she at the other.

"You know I have not yet met a man I can marry." She shook her head.

"Indeed, but surely one day you would like to provide an heir to your estate?"

"You wouldn't like to inherit it?"

"Certainly not. I have a big enough estate as it is, without yours. They are at opposite ends of the country too. Very inconvenient. I do hope you'll marry soon and not let me inherit. If you will do that for me, I would be much obliged."

"Very well, but if I marry, you must too."

"I will not. I have no desire to find some worthless female who simply wants a title."

"Choice words Philip." She shook a finger at him. "But one day you will find yourself in love and it will not be returned."

"I hope you're correct," he replied. "It will be what I deserve, I'm sure."

Louise looked up and saw that they were outside her house. It was one of many in Grosvenor Crescent, an exclusive part of London where the streets were wide and clean. Trees lined the pavement at equal distances and added to the overall feeling of affluence. The houses, usually with four stories, looked small from the outside, but opened up inside. With the kitchens in the basement and servants' quarters in the attic, there was ample space for the fashionable residents to live comfortably. Houses in this street were bought and sold at very inflated prices because of the prestige attached to them.

"When shall I see you again?" she asked with a playful smile, for she knew what the answer would be; it was always the same.

"I cannot say, but soon I'm sure." He kissed her hand.

"I look forward to it. Whenever that might be."

He let go of her hand, turned and made his way down the street. His steps were light and brisk. One of the things she liked the most about her friendship with Philip was its unpredictability. But even if she didn't see him again for a while, at least there was tomorrow's lecture to look forward to. Perhaps she might be lucky enough to see Charles Lucas again.

2

―――――

"It was very good of you to accompany me Jane, but there really was no need." Charles Lucas handed his sister down from the cab. The horse's hooves clattered on the cobbled street as it waited, impatient to be moving again.

"I know, but I'm eager to see what sort of man Mr Bagshawe is." Jane straightened her blue muslin dress and checked her bonnet.

He raised his eyebrows in query and closed the carriage door.

"I want to see what sort of man refused to give you an apprenticeship all those years ago," she explained.

"I'm grateful for your loyalty, Jane, but you mustn't hold it against Mr Bagshawe. He probably saw my potential to be a better engineer than him and decided he couldn't let me out-do him. Besides, I did well with Mr Sanderson, didn't I? My career would have taken a much different turn if I had been accepted into Mr Bagshawe's employment, and I don't mean in a good way."

"Is he that bad Charles?"

"Just wait and see."

Charles held out his arm and his sister took it. They entered the auditorium of the Institution of Civil Engineers and found two of the last remaining seats near the back. He mused that it was certainly less fraught being an audience member than a speaker. Yesterday's lecture had made him somewhat edgy and nervous beforehand, though he hoped he had hidden his fears. It wasn't that he wasn't used to public speaking, it was just that being asked by the Institute was something he didn't wish to make a muddle of. It had all gone smoothly, and now he sat back and relaxed, glad that yesterday was over with.

Not long after they were seated, the lecture began. They had arrived late because Charles had been lost in his work. It was a common occurrence though Jane had been prepared and reminded him several times before they left home.

Charles took a long look around the place. It was mostly gentlemen, as expected. A few sat with ladies who were most likely their wives. A few rows in front, he saw the same fashionable lady who was present yesterday at his lecture; the one who asked so many questions, and even sketched his bridge. What was her name again? He wracked his brain for a few moments. Miss Thomas. That was it.

Her enthusiasm had amused him somewhat though he hadn't thought of her again until now. It was unusual for a person such as her to take such a keen interest in his work, though he was becoming well known as an engineer since winning the bridge competition. He hadn't been asked so many questions since the interview with the judges. Yesterday after the lecture, he had looked at her with amused wonder as she chatted to the man who interrupted them. Being asked such questions from such a smart lady was a new sensation. She seemed more knowledgeable about such things than any other he had met with, even his own sister.

Ashton, his partner, had approached him immediately after he had escaped her questions. "What did Miss Thomas have to say to you?" he said in an excited voice.

"Miss Thomas?"

"Yes." Ashton raised his eyebrows in surprise and indicated to her. "That is the famous Miss Thomas."

"Famous Miss Thomas? I really had no idea." Charles said in a nonchalant voice. He vaguely recalled the name.

"Don't give me that Charles. You must have heard of her – everyone in the engineering field has." He paused a moment, then said in a panicked voice, "I hope you were not rude to her? I was rather hoping this year we would be invited to her annual Engineers' Dinner. The invitations haven't been sent out yet."

So that is where he had heard the name before. Charles took a step back and regarded his partner, his face incredulous.

"Of course I wasn't rude to her. I was pleasantness itself. But I do not think you should expect to be invited if you have never even spoken to her."

Ashton relaxed. "Yes, exactly. I know how you generally dislike the gentry, but on this occasion you must not let it manifest itself in your behaviour to her, of all people."

"I only dislike them because they get in the way of my work. They look down on me and those like me. I have met too many who have tried to stop progress because they are scared of change and don't like the lower classes earning an honest living." Charles shifted about then continued, "I will never forget how Mr Rustling and his cronies tried to call a halt to so many of my replacement railway bridges. And for what reason? Nothing else than to cause trouble because they had nothing better to do with their time. They are all the same."

Ashton rolled his eyes. "You must try and stop thinking about Mr Rustling, it will only make you irritable for the rest of the day. But Miss Thomas is very beautiful, is she not?" he said, his voice suddenly soft. "I'd been told by many that she was lovely, but I never believed it was true. I just thought people exaggerated it due to her wealth."

Charles relaxed his shoulders and noticed how Ashton's dark eyes scanned Miss Thomas. She was certainly the sort of woman a man's eyes were naturally drawn to. "Yes, I suppose she is uncommonly pleasing to look at." She was moderately tall, and with dark hair the colour of jet. His eyes were drawn to her figure, which curved in the right places. There was nothing wanting in her appearance.

"Uncommonly pleasing to look at!" Ashton had scoffed. "You really must learn how to appreciate the female form Charles."

"I assure you I'm quite capable of doing that," he responded.

His mind wandered back to the present, and Mr Bagshawe's steady, condescending voice at the lecture. Occasionally, his glance would fall upon Miss Thomas, and as time wore on, he became more absorbed in watching her reaction to what Mr Bagshawe said. He noticed she wrote things in her notebook, and sometimes, from what he could see of her face, for he was slightly to the left of her, her brow would contract in a frown. Several times he saw her shake her head and mutter, then sigh heavily. He glanced at his sister. Jane noticed none of it. If she was bored, she showed no sign, her blue eyes fixed on the speaker at the front.

When Mr Bagshawe finished speaking, the floor was

opened for questions, and Charles immediately waited for Miss Thomas to ask her question first, in the same way as yesterday. She was beaten to it by a gentleman near the back. One corner of his mouth was pulled into a slight smile as he saw frustration etched on her face.

Then at last there was silence after the question was answered. He watched and waited as she put up her hand.

"Mr Bagshawe, all you have done this afternoon is talk about your career and those who have opposed you in your plans to build the sewer system. Why have you not explained the sewer design fully?" she asked in a crisp voice.

Mr Bagshawe's jaw dropped, his face went red and he spluttered, "I'm sorry madam, I do not have the time left to explain the design."

"Clearly, because you couldn't stop talking about yourself!" She crossed her arms.

There was a deathly hush throughout the place.

Mr Bagshawe pulled at the bottom of his waistcoat and his abundant mustache twitched. "The plans are available at the central library, and they are too complicated for most to understand." He dismissed her with a wave of his arm.

"I'm sure most of the people present, including myself, will take great offence at that remark. And if we wanted to know about your career and those who oppose you, we could have read it in the Times! You seem to like to print a letter complaining about them every week."

"Madam please! I have never heard such insolence. I came here out of the goodness of my heart, not to put up with such audacity."

"Well I for one would rather you had stayed at home, for you have wasted my time. I may as well have asked a beggar in the street outside to explain the sewer system for all I have learned today."

With that, Mr Bagshawe became bright red, and shook a little. He refrained from speaking further and they stared at each other for a long moment. Then a gentleman standing at the side stepped forward and coughed to bring everyone to attention. "The Institution of Civil Engineers would like to thank Mr Bagshawe for coming today and speaking." He began to clap and the sound of faint applause from came from one or two others in the audience, then stopped.

Charles turned to his sister. "Jane, what do you think of that? I have never seen anyone look so angry, it took all the self will I could muster not to laugh at him."

"It was a shame they had to have such a public argument, but I feel that the lady was right, I was so bored halfway through I had to stop myself from yawning aloud. He does seem to be full of his own self-importance."

Charles agreed. "He is well known in engineering circles to be arrogant. Do you see now why I'm glad I wasn't his apprentice?"

Jane placed a reassuring hand on her brother's arm. "You had a lucky escape indeed."

They drifted out of the hall among the throng of people, and outside saw Miss Thomas waiting for her carriage. A moment later, they were joined by Ashton.

"I didn't realise you were here," Charles commented to his partner. "How did you enjoy the lecture?"

"I wasn't in the lecture. I came for one reason, and one reason only." He turned to look in front and pointed. "I thought Miss Thomas would be here, and I was right. Charles, go and speak to her and I will approach shortly afterwards. You can introduce us." Ashton adjusted his cravat and smoothed his hand over his brown hair.

Charles's eyes widened in disbelief. "I will do no such thing."

Ashton sighed. "Charles, you're not thinking. Sometimes I need you to help me advance our contacts. Miss Thomas will be a very advantageous acquaintance to have. Please do as I ask."

The stared at each other for a few moments, until Charles dropped his shoulders and relented.

"Very well, for the partnership I will do it."

"Good. Now quickly, before she is gone." Ashton shooed him away and he walked over to Miss Thomas before he changed his mind. He presented himself with a small bow.

"I hope you do not mind my impertinence at approaching you, but I wished to say that you were kinder to me yesterday than you were to Mr Bagshawe a moment ago," he said, smiling a little. He watched her reaction, hoping for a positive response and noticed she faltered for a moment.

"I'm sorry to have said things in the heat of the moment," she commented in a serious voice. "I do not like having my time wasted by such arrogance and conceit."

"Mr Bagshawe is well known for those attributes."

"Yes, I have heard. But all I know is that he didn't deserve to speak today. I was disappointed. Out of the three, yours was the only lecture worth attending."

"Thank you," he replied in a sincere tone, and was secretly pleased.

She stared at him for a moment as though taking in his features and it unnerved him a little. Her gaze was confident and easy, her eyes clear and expressive. He wondered what to say next, and cursed Ashton for insisting he do this. He was never one for idle chit-chat, especially with people he didn't know.

Especially with a woman.

He glanced over to Ashton and his sister, but they were deep in conversation and he couldn't get their attention.

He was relieved when Miss Thomas spoke. "I was sorry we were interrupted from speaking yesterday after the lecture," she said.

"You were?" He tried to disguise the surprise in his voice.

"I still have many questions to ask about the bridge design."

"Ah." He nodded, and noticed she looked at him with anticipation.

"Then I hope you will have the opportunity to ask me more shortly. In the meantime, allow me to introduce my sister, Miss Jane Lucas, and my partner, Mr Ashton." He indicated to where the pair were standing, and they moved over to them.

The introductions were made and Jane greeted Miss Thomas with openness, but any conversation between them was thwarted by Ashton, who interrupted straight away. He took Miss Thomas's hand and refused to let it go.

"May I take this opportunity, Miss Thomas, of saying what a pleasure it is to meet you. I have been looking for a chance to make your acquaintance for a long time." Charles rolled his eyes at Ashton's sudden politeness and courtesy. The usually rough and plain-speaking man was clearly trying to impress. Charles hoped he wouldn't babble too much.

"You have?" Miss Thomas pulled her hand away from Ashton's hard grasp.

"Of course. The name of Thomas is well known and respected amongst the engineering world," he said through a grin.

Charles let his mind drift as he heard Ashton's words rattle on. Miss Thomas was polite and gave the appearance of being pleased and interested in what Ashton said. He suspected she was hiding her true feelings. Eventually, when Ashton paused for breath, Miss Thomas turned to Jane.

"Miss Lucas, I'm pleased to meet you. Did you attend the lecture today with your brother?"

Jane squared her petite shoulders as she was suddenly the centre of attention. "Yes, and I thought you were right in everything you said to Mr Bagshawe. I took an instant dislike to him."

They continued to talk of the lecture and then of London. After five minutes of conversation, it was clear to all of them that the two ladies had taken an instant liking to each other.

"Are you attending the final lecture tomorrow?" Jane asked her. "I promised Charles I would sit with him, but after today I think I may try and avoid it."

A glint of humour crossed Charles's face, it was so typical of Jane. "She makes it sound like I forced her to come, but it was her idea."

"I do intend to come to the lecture tomorrow," Miss Thomas said, amused at brother and sister. "But if you can spare your sister afterwards, Mr Lucas, would you allow her to come to tea?"

"Of course," he replied and tried to ignore the look of glee on Ashton's face.

"That is most gracious of you. Thank you," Jane replied. "My mother will be more than happy for me to call."

"Your mother? She must come too," Miss Thomas said, the tone of her voice implying that she wouldn't take no for an answer.

Miss Thomas's carriage pulled up and Charles watched as Ashton eagerly took the role of helping her safely into her carriage; he bowed deeply over her hand as they bid farewell.

They stood and watched the carriage pull away. Ashton mumbled to Charles, "Maybe the best route to that acquaintance is through your sister. You'd better nurture it as much as you can."

"You ask too much. How can I cultivate such a thing? Friendships between women are a mystery to me. You had better leave me to my bridge."

He was about to walk away when Ashton put a restraining hand on his arm. "Do what you can." Then he added, "For the partnership, and an invitation to the Engineers' Dinner. We must cultivate our connections, especially now your reputation is growing."

"Very well. But try and give me more warning next time you want me to make a fool of myself."

. . .

Jane and her mother arrived on time the next day. From the first floor window Louise watched them as they alighted from the carriage and she ran down the stairs to prepare herself to greet them. When they entered they couldn't have guessed at her previous exertion.

Louise was eager to impress them because they were Mr Lucas's relatives. She had been surprised but pleased when Mr Lucas had approached and spoken to her yesterday. No, not totally surprised; he had introduced his partner who was clearly the reason behind him speaking to her. She couldn't be annoyed at Mr Lucas for his so obvious introduction and for some reason she felt she could forgive him a great many things and she wasn't sure why. One thing was certain, she had taken an instant liking to Jane Lucas. She envied her having such a brother, and one so talented in his field.

Louise's house was by no means small, though not the largest in the vicinity. Like so many town houses, it was terraced, with six marbled steps leading to a covered porch-way supported by four pillars. Inside there was a library, which Louise added to frequently. The dining room was small compared to Glazebrook's, but the walnut table was crafted with such care, it suited the room perfectly. The bedchambers numbered only five but were large enough to be comfortable. During any stay in London she occupied one of the smaller rooms at the back of the house away from the noise of the street.

The ladies were shown into the drawing room, where Louise waited in anticipation.

"Miss Lucas, I'm very pleased to see you again," she said the moment Jane entered.

"And I you," she replied. "This is my mother."

Mrs Lucas curtsied and Louise was surprised at how small she was. Despite her stature, she seemed to dominate the room. She didn't look much older than fifty and although her hair was grey, her eyes were bright blue.

"This drawing room is delightful!" Mrs Lucas seated herself next to Louise on the sofa.

"Thank you," said Louise. "Though I cannot take praise for a room I didn't decorate or furnish."

"Who was it?"

"My mother."

"Well then, she had similar tastes to me. That red silk wallpaper is exactly as I would choose."

Conversation, as was inevitable in such situations of new acquaintance, then turned to the weather.

Once this line of dialogue was exhausted, the tea arrived, and as soon as they were comfortably sipping their refreshment, Mrs Lucas began to ask more questions of her hostess.

"Jane tells me you attended Charles's lecture and that you have a great interest in engineering."

"Yes," Louise replied over her teacup, secretly pleased that the conversation had quickly gone in the direction she hoped. "It was very enlightening."

"I'm so proud of Charles," Mrs Lucas said. "He may be the younger son, but I think he has already achieved more than his older brother."

"You have two sons?"

"Yes, Edward is two years older than Charles. He is a lawyer here in London, a partner in a well-respected company, Finch Associates. Have you heard of them?"

"No, I'm afraid not."

"Well, they are on the other side of town, and though their clients are respectable, they are perhaps not in such high circles as you."

Jane placed her teacup down. "Mama, Edward has achieved much as well." She turned to Louise. "My mother professes not to have a favourite child, but I fear sometimes her guard is let down and her preference for Charles shows itself." A teasing smile played on Jane's lips.

"Well Jane, you always say that, and I always deny it! I love all my three children, and although I have an excellent relationship with them, it's Charles who is most like their father. Is that the preference you speak of?"

"How long have you been a widow?" Louise asked.

"Nearly ten years now. I miss Walter greatly."

Louise looked away as all-too-familiar memories of loss flooded through her. "Although I have never lost a husband, I do know what it's like to lose a loved one."

"You have no family living, I hear?"

Louise surmised that her reputation preceded her. It wasn't uncommon for new acquaintances to know at least a few basic facts about her. Some knew far too much, and others heard many untruths. She hoped the Lucas family fell into the first group. "Not my immediate family, no. I have a cousin and aunt and a few other distant relatives. Second cousins and such."

Jane looked a little shocked. "I'm sorry for it, truly I am. But you have many friends, do you not?"

"Yes. I'm lucky in that respect, and my cousin, Lord Philip, is a great help and support to me." Louise shifted about, she desired a change in the conversation. She was not willing to dwell on what she didn't have, and the loneliness so often felt. "You both live with Charles and not your eldest?"

"Yes," Mrs Lucas answered, even though the question had been directed at Jane. "We're very fond of Edward and his wife Rose, but they have four children and enough to keep them occupied without extra family getting in the way."

Louise nodded. "Perhaps one day Mr Lucas will marry, and then what will you do?"

Jane gave a kind of snort. "Charles is far too busy to think of marrying, I'm sure of it. He works too hard and too long hours to meet any eligible women. Despite our efforts to the contrary."

Mrs Lucas glared at her daughter for a moment. "What Jane means is that Charles has yet to meet a woman he admires enough to marry. When that happens, we will review the living arrangements. Hopefully he will marry someone who will be like a daughter to me, and then there wouldn't be a problem."

"I'm sure I shall be married before him," Jane said. "And Mama you can come and live with me."

"You're very kind Jane. But we'll see." Mother and daughter exchanged a tender glance, as silence fell on the room. Louise admired their obvious affection for each other. To have a mother living would be a wondrous thing indeed.

Louise was broken from her reveries by Mrs Lucas's soft voice. "Dare I ask – are you free tomorrow night? We're having a dinner with only a few select friends and would be honoured if you would come. But I must warn you now, we're not grand by any means. However, I can guarantee hearty food and excellent company."

"I have no prior engagements tomorrow evening and the honour would be mine."

The ladies stayed another half an hour. All three felt a mutual but silent affirmation that they would like to continue the acquaintance.

Mrs Lucas, although not usually dazzled by wealth, felt Miss Thomas a worthy friend for her daughter and as they were traveling home remarked, "Jane, if you wish to become friends with Miss Thomas, I would be glad of it."

"Do you think she likes me as much as I like her?"

"I think she does. But you're so lovely, who cannot but help liking you?"

"If you continue like this, I shall start to think I'm your favourite child," Jane smiled. She looked out of the carriage window. "I confess, I was a little overwhelmed by the grandeur of her house and her wealth. I think she is very rich. Did you see the silver in the cabinet? It must be worth hundreds of pounds."

"But she is unlike so many of the wealthy," Mrs Lucas agreed. "She is unassuming and easy to talk to. Not officious and perfectly amiable. Yes, I like her very much."

"I didn't see anything eccentric about her," Jane agreed. "The gossips who like to whisper about her must just be jealous."

"Indeed. I have heard whispers that Miss Thomas is brazen and assertive. I saw nothing of the sort. They must be envious of her wealth and independence."

3

─────

If the Lucas women were happy with their new acquaintance, it was nothing to the feelings Louise held in return. Though she was something of a social butterfly with many acquaintances especially in London, she felt the Lucas women were different from typical ladies.

Jane was a lovely girl in her own right and had obviously been brought up well-educated and informed. She was sure that their friendship, if cultivated, would be mutually beneficial. It was true that part of Jane's appeal was the family surname she bore, but Louise could see a depth to her that was missing from so many women. She was a little surprised that Jane wasn't already married; those men in her social circle must surely see her accomplishments? Perhaps there already was an attachment that Louise wasn't aware of.

Likewise, Mrs Lucas was an excellent woman. She showed great affection for her children, and clearly nurtured their individuality. In her eyes, they could do no wrong. Louise thought this the perfect attitude for a parent to have, and thereby rendered the children a freedom that wasn't often afforded many in their day and age. Certainly,

Louise's own wealth, though a great benefit, and something others clearly coveted, was an encumbrance to her at times. Her responsibilities were so many that sometimes she felt at a loss to cope on her own. Every decision she made was done to the best of her ability, but she longed for a consistent mentor or companion to share the burden. Philip was a dependable help when she felt overwhelmed. What would she do without his assistance? But she hardly ever saw him, and despite the fact that he would always answer her letters, he was so often away around the country that his replies were inevitably delayed.

That afternoon and evening, though busy with engagements, she forced herself to stop any thoughts of the pressures of her wealth, and instead turned her mind to the dinner the following evening. There was a deep pleasure she barely acknowledged even to herself: she was glad that she would have the opportunity to speak to Mr Lucas again. But she must not let her friendship with Jane be guided by her wish to see the brother. It would be shameful and a disservice to Jane to use her in such a way.

When the following evening arrived, she was late dressing. A letter from her steward arrived while her maid was arranging her hair. It wasn't in her nature to ignore business letters, and she dismissed the maid for a short time, and sat at her dressing table to read it.

Her eyes scanned the letter to take in the major details. There was flooding in the fields near the Axe river again, but that was to be expected – it happened every year. It made many of the fields unusable through the winter, but in the summer when the weather was drier and the river flow subsided, the grass was all the sweeter for the flooding.

The Turner brothers had been at each other's throats again; this time it was a border dispute over their adjoining farms. She sighed to herself. If she had a sibling alive, she wouldn't argue like them. She would cherish each moment. But she remembered one of the lessons her father taught her: people from all stations in life never appreciate what they have. She had always been determined not to be one of them, especially every time she passed a starving child in the street. Every day she knew how lucky she was to be able to put food into her mouth.

The harvest was almost over, with only the last apples to be collected. Preparations for the fair were nearly complete. She would return for that, and never missed it. She remembered the smiling faces and the laughter above the musicians. The rows of stalls selling foods of all kinds.

Her maid re-entered the room and broke her from her thoughts, and she continued to dress. Thoughts of home would have to be left for later and in a way she was glad; her home in Devon stood empty – empty of family at least.

Despite the late business and reduced time to dress, her carriage pulled up outside the Lucas house exactly on time. She was happy with her outfit, having chosen a cream satin evening dress together with a simple pearl necklace, matching earrings and a green Indian shawl that gave her outfit colour. Though she dressed carefully, she didn't wear one of her best dresses. She wanted to fit into her surroundings and look becoming but not stand out or intimidate her hosts.

She stepped out of the carriage and took a long glance at the Lucas house. She was surprised at the size and situation of it. It was a new building, a few years old, in the middle of a long row of terraces. The road, though not as wide and clean as her own, was still very respectable. The red brick went up to three floors, as well as an attic room. The front entrance, though not majestic, held a certain simplistic charm. The Lucases were wealthier than she had originally supposed and she made a mental note to enquire what business the late Walter Lucas had been in. Since the eldest son was a lawyer, it was likely that had been his profession. Her knowledge of the Lucas and Ashton partnership meant that it was unlikely Charles Lucas took home a large salary each year. Most up and coming engineers, though revered and respected, lived on a small wage.

Inside, she was welcomed by Mrs Lucas, who took hold of her hand warmly. "My dear Miss Thomas, you look radiant tonight. I'm so pleased you're here. Come into the drawing room." She was led to a door to the left. The room was small, like the rest of the house and the heat from the fireplace engulfed it. The oil lamps were lit, even though it wasn't dark outside, and gave it a hospitable glow. Louise felt strangely at home.

The whole family were assembled to receive their guests and she was glad to see that Charles Lucas was present, as well as his older brother Edward, and Edward's wife, Rose.

When the introductions were over, Rose Lucas quickly drew Louise aside into conversation.

"I'm delighted to meet you," Rose said. "I've heard all about you from Jane."

Unfortunately, Louise couldn't say the same. But, she noted, Rose was a bright, young, attractive woman. Much younger than her husband, with dark auburn hair and blue eyes. She was an attentive listener, agreeing and nodding in an exaggerated manner to anything Louise said, and was obviously impressed with her. She was so nice that Louise could do nothing but feel welcome and attended to, and though she was the centre of attention, she didn't mind. She was used to it.

A few minutes later some other guests were shown in:

Mr and Mrs Hunter and their daughter Constance, a quiet, shy girl of nineteen. Constance appeared to be a family favourite, especially with Rose, who greeted her like a sister with an affectionate kiss on each cheek.

"My dear Contstance, let me be the lucky one to introduce you to Miss Louise Thomas."

She pulled the girl over to Louise and instigated a conversation between them. Louise was used to small chit-chat, and when she applied herself could make the quietest people speak. Constance Hunter was no different, and though at first she spoke only the odd word, she soon began to open up under Louise's expert questioning. Rose continued to nod and make the odd comment when she could, smiling broadly as she did. A few times Louise did feel trapped talking to this girl, when she would much rather be on the other side of the room. She glanced several times at Jane, Charles and Mrs Lucas, who all stood together, but to no avail. They were all busy talking to each other and how could they tell that Louise wanted to speak to them? She was excellent at hiding her true feelings.

Her saviour came in the form of Mr Ashton, who arrived fifteen minutes later. He burst in out of breath, with his cravat looking as though it had been hastily tied. Everyone stopped talking and turned to look at him.

"At last!" Mrs Lucas said. "We thought you would never arrive, and we have Miss Thomas here tonight too. I know you were looking forward to speaking to her again."

Mr Ashton looked at Louise and she raised her eyebrows in query.

"Of course, I'm very sorry to be late," Mr Ashton stepped forward to greet Louise. He bowed deeply, fluttered compliments such as "delighted", "affable company", "guest of honour". A quick glance around the room showed several of the other men, including Charles, with amused looks on their faces. Louise suppressed a feeling of awkwardness. She didn't like being the centre of attention when she was an object of ridicule.

After nearly fifteen minutes of speaking to Mr Ashton, who wouldn't let Louise speak to anyone else, dinner was announced and finally she got her chance to talk to Charles. He sat at the top of the table, and she was most fortunately placed next to him.

At the first opportunity, Louise turned to him. "I was sorry our conversation ended so quickly the day of your lecture. As I mentioned yesterday, I have further things to ask you." Her voice was soft and she tried to hide her eagerness.

He looked at her with a faint hint of intrigue. "I thought you might not miss this opportunity. Have you been analysing what I said all these days?"

"A little, but you need not worry, I'll not get into an argument with you." She tried to stop herself smiling.

"You haven't brought your notebook – can you remember all the questions?"

"Of course, though do not assume I haven't concealed my notebook about my person."

He inclined his head, indicating Louise should begin her questions. She felt awkward though as she did, especially as they were uninterrupted by the other guests as they discussed the bridge. Though several of the others seated nearby listened into their conversation, none were able to join in, such was the intensity of their discourse.

Eventually, Charles's attention was taken away from Louise by Mr Waters, who was seated opposite. Louise didn't mind, as she was seated next to Jane, and felt she had neglected her new friend. But her thoughts remained on

Charles. She was even more impressed with him than ever. His depth of knowledge was outstanding, adding to his other appealing attributes. Those, she was not sure she should think about too much.

Later on, she was engaged in much conversation with Mr Ashton, who was nearly opposite her and listened to much of the previous talk. He continually spoke of engineering topics, but she decided Mr Lucas was the only man she would talk to on that subject, so she expertly steered the conversation to other matters. Quickly she found out about Mr Ashton. He was forty-five years old, widowed a few years ago with no children. She also discovered that while he was the administrator of the partnership and dealt with the day-to-day things, it was Mr Lucas who was the engineering brain, just as she had heard.

When it was time for the ladies to leave the room, Mr Ashton prevented Louise from going for a moment.

"It's a shame you must leave now, I was enjoying our conversation so much. We must continue shortly, I don't think we will be long."

"Indeed," Louise said. She rose from her seat and pushed the chair in, and though she liked Ashton, hoped that she would be able to speak more with Mr Lucas.

"One more thing," Ashton said. "You come from Devonshire I hear?"

"Yes."

"Do you happen to know a gentleman from that county called Mr Robert Adams?"

Louise grabbed the back of the chair as a moment of blind panic washed over her, and then she forced herself to answer. "Why, I . . . I have heard of him yes. Why do you ask?"

"Merely that he is a major investor in our partnership,

but whenever we ask to meet him, he refuses. I wondered; have you met him?"

"Yes. Yes I know him," she swallowed. "I know him – quite well." She couldn't look Mr Ashton in the eye, and stared at the painting of a woman on the wall behind him, who had an annoyingly serene expression on her face. "He is the sort of man who prefers to keep himself to himself, if you understand my meaning?"

Ashton gave a curt nod.

She continued on, though she wasn't sure why. She should have escaped the room before his questions continued. "You have never had a problem communicating with Mr Adams? That is, he always answers your correspondence in a timely manner?"

"Yes, we've never had any issues in that respect. It's just that with all our investors we like to try and meet them. He is the only major one we haven't met. He must be a very busy man."

"Yes, I believe he is. But Mr Adams does not like to meet his investments in person, he prefers hard facts and financial reports. Trust me, you're likely to receive a rebuff every time you ask to see him in person."

"I will remember that, thank you. You seem to know a lot about him? For someone so unavailable I mean"

Louise glanced at the other men in the room. They were all staring at her. She blushed under the sudden scrutiny. It was time to leave.

She shut the dining room door behind her and sighed, pausing outside to gain her composure. For some reason, she held her ear against the door to try to hear the conversation going on in the dining room, but no sound penetrated out. She lifted her hand to her cheek. It was burning, she must be bright red. Why hadn't she been able to hide her agitation more?

After a few moments she decided a distraction was what she needed and she went to the drawing room to join the other ladies.

"I do apologise for not leaving the dining room with you all," she said to no one in particular. "Mr Ashton wouldn't let me go." she gave a small nervous laugh and cringed at the sound of it. "Sometimes I get so engrossed in conversations I forget where I am."

"Do not worry yourself," Jane linked her arm and lead her to the tea and coffee table. "I was about to come and rescue you – but here, would you like some tea?"

Louise took the cup and saucer from Jane and sipped it quickly. It was a little too cold for her liking, but she was grateful for the liquid to sooth her dry throat. She didn't allow herself any time for reflection on her parting words with Mr Ashton, but she chastened herself for not being ready for such questions. She should have known it was likely that Robert Adams's name would be mentioned tonight, but she had so far passed the evening so pleasantly she had let her guard drop. Indeed, the assembled family and guests made the evening most enchanting. She hoped that her hesitation in answering about Mr Adams hadn't betrayed anything. Her mind ran over the conversation again. No, she was sure they could suspect nothing. Why would they? She was being ridiculous.

Louise stood next to Jane and Miss Hunter and they spoke of the house and of the area in London. Jane didn't appear to be as fond of Constance Hunter as Rose. She noticed the somewhat quiet Miss Hunter joined in with much conversation until the gentlemen came into the room, when she withdrew herself into a quiet corner on her own. She put it down to her age.

Louise was excused from further conversation with Mr Ashton when Jane pulled him away and demanded his opinion on some books she had recently purchased. A swift glance at her showed it was purposely orchestrated. A few moments later, Louise was approached by Edward Lucas. He was in looks similar to his younger brother, but it became clear that in personality he was very different. He had a seriousness about him that Louise didn't often come across and took every comment she made to him in an austere manner. Her playful comments, so often well-received in such social occasions, seemed to have no effect on him. Louise, an expert at conversation, managed to steer the dialogue towards Charles by explaining how she became acquainted with the family and in a few minutes found herself face to face with Charles again. Edward, still standing beside them both, asked Louise, "It's unusual for a woman to be so interested in engineering, how did you get such an enthusiasm?"

Louise hesitated for a moment. Should she reveal why? Would they be interested? More importantly, would they think her a simpleton? Despite her initial wish to evade the subject, she began to speak.

"When I was a girl, I traveled to Portsmouth with my father. He had business there, and decided to take me. One day on our way through the town, we walked to the river, where a new bridge was being built. I was fascinated by the construction scene. It wasn't a very big bridge, the river was low, and they were about halfway through. My father and I watched for some time, and in the end he dragged me away. I longed to watch more, and a few days later, my father took me back to see it. Ever since that day, I've had a great interest in engineering of all kinds, not only bridges."

She turned to Charles. "I still wonder how gentlemen such as yourself can contrive to think how to achieve such feats. I sometimes wish I had been born a boy. I'm sure I would have pursued a career in engineering."

Louise felt herself flush for a moment. She was rambling. She glanced at Charles, who was watching her. Then she looked away, unable to meet his gaze any longer, knowing she had exposed something private, something she rarely spoke of. Did he sense that?

"I can understand your enthusiasm," he said in a serious tone and after a long pause.

"You can?" she looked up at him again, grateful for not being laughed at.

"Yes, I had a similar experience. But I was a little older and at school. One of the masters arranged for a ship builder to visit us. He was an old pupil of the school, and only a few of us who showed aptitude in the sciences were allowed to listen. He talked to us about the process of designing and building ships, and from that moment on I knew the career I wanted."

"You haven't designed any ships though?"

"None that have been constructed, but I have, in my own time, designed many." He smiled, "Some made of paper for my nephews, and some made of wood as Christmas presents. But maybe one day I will design something bigger." His voice drifted off and he took a sip of coffee.

Louise was amused at the thought of him sitting at an office desk making wooden boats. He was lucky to have nephews, and they were even luckier children to have such an uncle.

"Did your father oppose your decision to be an engineer?" she asked, and noticed that Edward moved away to the other side of the room.

"At first he did. He wanted me to be a lawyer like him, but I persisted in asking his approval to train as an engineer and he relented. My mother helped persuade him. She was always able to if she put her mind to it. Or so she tells me."

"An ideal mother then."

They both turned and looked at Mrs Lucas. She was standing at the other side of the room behind a small table that held the tea things, smiling and fussing, making sure all the guests were being seen to. She must have sensed Louise and Charles looking at her because she glanced across and acknowledged them with a nod.

"She is very proud of you."

"She told you that?"

"Yes, but you need not be embarrassed. I think you're very lucky to have your mother still living. I can hardly remember mine."

"How old were you when she died?"

"Ten."

"My father died when I was twenty, so I still have fond memories of him."

"I was also twenty when my father died."

Louise thought this commonality between them a little morbid, and in a bid to change the subject to something brighter asked, "Has you mother never thought about re-marrying?"

"Not that I'm aware of. But if she chose to do that, I would be happy for her. I think my father would have wanted it."

"But you take care of her for now."

"Yes."

Their gaze drifted over to Mrs Lucas again. She was busy

again with serving her guests. Lucky woman, Louise thought.

. . .

Charles looked at his pocket watch. It was quarter to eleven and only fifteen minutes until the carriages arrived to take the guests away. This evening hadn't been too taxing. He felt sure he had done as Ashton instructed him; be amiable, polite and affable to Miss Thomas. In fact, he admired her intellect and her sharp observations. It was a shame she was gentry, otherwise he might be at liberty to admire her more. They had spoken for a further half hour and discussed the finer points of the growing steel industry in Sheffield, the working conditions of the steel workers, the quality of the steel needed for his bridge over the Tamar and the effort required to transport it from Yorkshire to Devon.

He tucked his watch away and took in the room with a single rapid glance. Miss Hunter was talking to Rose, instructing her in some sort of needlework. His sister and Miss Thomas were seated by the fire, deep in conversation. Edward moved to speak to Mr Ashton near the window and from the looks of it, they were discussing the port they were drinking.

His mother approached and whispered, "Miss Thomas and Jane seem to have become firm friends. She must be pleased with Jane, but then who wouldn't be? Mr Hunter said earlier that although she is famous for her Engineers' Dinner, she does not usually court new friends."

"What else does Mr Hunter say about her?"

"Nothing much."

He gave his mother an enquiring look.

"Very well," she relented. "You always seem to know when I'm keeping things back. He also said that she is very rich and has a large estate in Devonshire."

"That much we knew already."

"And that she is the richest woman in Devon."

He looked at Miss Thomas again, who was laughing at something Jane said. She was one of the more open and amenable of the gentry he had met. But he had a suspicion she could be as equally awkward as the others if she chose to be. It seemed as though she was one of the more open-minded of her class.

"Are you pleased with Jane's new friend?" asked his mother, tentatively.

He thought for a moment. "She is a little unusual. She is knowledgeable."

His mother scoffed. "Always the engineer, even in your description of a lady."

"What do you mean? What's wrong with my description?"

"Knowledgeable! Unusual! She is by far the best woman I have met in years."

"Do you think she is a good influence on Jane?" Charles said, ignoring his mother's comments.

"I'm sure I don't know what you mean. How can she be a bad influence? She is a genteel lady, and I'm glad they are becoming friends. I know your view of the gentry. We're well aware of your dislike of the intrusive way in which they conduct their business – especially after Mr Rustling – but she really is a most pleasing woman and unlike those that you claim to disapprove of so much."

"I shall not stop Jane having any friend you approve of."

Mrs Lucas gave a curt nod. "I'm a good judge of character, after all."

Despite his words, he took a moment to fully evaluate the two friends sat at the fire. Both were confident and sanguine. Jane was blonde and pretty, smaller than Miss

Thomas, and her face had the glow of youth. He wondered how old Miss Thomas was, and decided that she was probably almost thirty. She was still beautiful though, her black hair expertly tied in the latest fashion. Her brown eyes reflected the light and he noticed a gentle ease about her that she hadn't shown before, especially in those moments when he studied her at Mr Bagshawe's lecture, or even at the dinner table as they spoke. But he shook himself. Her beauty wasn't the greatest he had noticed amongst the women of his acquaintance. Perhaps, like many others who are admired for their beauty, such compliments lay in an underlying knowledge of the lady's wealth.

She had interesting conversation though, and certainly knew more than most women and men. He didn't object to that. He disliked stupid women. No, he was sure his examination of her was more than just functional. He could admire a woman just for being a woman, like most men did.

Ashton was one of those men who was obviously dazzled by her wealth, and had been most adamant that they should entertain and flatter this woman so that they received an invitation to her Engineers' Dinner.

He was interrupted from these reflections by Ashton murmuring in his ear, "I wonder if your sister's new friend would be interested in our more recent investment opportunities?"

Charles's eyes narrowed. "I'll leave all the investments to you, unless you want to start designing bridges."

"No fear! But you cannot blame me for asking."

"Good. But I doubt if she would be interested, despite her interest in engineering, I get the impression she wouldn't want to risk her money on such things. She's certainly never spoken about such things to me tonight, has she you?"

"No. We've only had the one conversation anyway, and I certainly wouldn't raise such an issue after the first few meetings, and to a lady. Whatever her elevated station in life."

Charles stepped away from Ashton. His partner's continual and unabated pursuit of funding made him weary at times. He knew his partner's work was equally important as his own; without the money he wouldn't be able to do any work. But he hated it when Ashton brought it so obviously into his own home.

. . .

When Louise arrived home, she was sorry that the evening ended even though she was exhausted. The journey home in the carriage only took twenty minutes, but she didn't allow herself the opportunity to think over all that was said, preferring to wait until she was safely inside her bedroom. It was unfortunate that Robert Adams was mentioned, but luckily it had only been for a short time and he hadn't been mentioned again. As her maid helped her undress, she reflected on the events of the night, the closeness of the family, the interdependency they often exhibited in small gestures to one another and the ease with which they talked made her suddenly aware of being alone. Although it never worried her much these days because she had come accustomed to it, tonight for the first time she wanted to be part of a family such as that. To have a brother, a sister, a mother. She closed her eyes as she sat at her dressing table, and for the first time she could remember, she imagined herself married. Yes, she wanted to be part of a family such as the Lucases, but it wasn't simply the family that drew her in – it was him. Charles Lucas. To be his wife, to share his family, to end the loneliness, was all she could think of. To be loved by him would be wonderful.

4

———————

The next day, Louise tried not to dwell on the feelings that surfaced the previous night and kept her awake for many hours. She wasn't often one to linger over such things and learnt a long time ago to suppress many of those wishes and desires she may have. It was her duty as mistress – the sole responsibility of her estate as the prominent reason for her self-inflicted self-denial. But still . . . however she tried to suppress her growing feelings, a part of her couldn't help but indulge in those sentiments.

She dressed wearily, tired due to lack of sleep. She snapped at her maid, but later after breakfast apologised to her. It wasn't Sophie's fault that she was fighting her feelings. She dreaded turning into one of those matriarchal women who treated her servants no better than slaves.

She had felt attraction to men before, but the spark of admiration had been there from the moment she saw him. Almost before she met him. The expectation of meeting the man she had heard so much about had been immense. She admired his work as an engineer, but the man himself proved to be every bit as attractive as the work he did.

For the first time she felt stupid; his intellect frightened her. But she tried not to shy away from his brilliance. It was endearing, and coupled with his caring attitude to his family, there was very little not to admire.

She was due to see Jane again that morning, but excused herself with a note, and pleaded a headache. Her mind was too clouded, and seeing the sister would only serve as a reminder of the brother.

A note written in a clear neat hand was returned within an hour of it having been sent:

Dear Louise,

I hope your ailment is temporary and that you will soon be better. I will go to the drapers this morning anyway and tell you when I next see you if the pink silk we talked of is as pretty as Miss Hunter said.

Yours etc.

Jane Lucas

After the morning alone, her state of mind was no better. She now regretted having cancelled her arrangements with Jane and decided to walk out for a while. She began to wonder what her late father would have said about it all. Would he approve of such a man as Mr Lucas?

There was no doubt he would understand her attraction to an engineer. From an early age, her father made many friends with those in trade and the professions. He had never, like many of his peers, shunned those who earned their money through hard work and expertise. Many were visitors to Glazebrook, including some of the top engineers, and as a girl, Louise had never been kept away from their company.

The last night her father had been alive, she kept a vigil

beside him, not willing to be away from him for one second before the inevitable happened. His illness had been mercifully quick, and he slipped in and out of consciousness many times. Each time he would instruct her, or sometimes he would call out his wife's name. In the early hours of his last morning he said to her:

"If you marry, make sure he won't use you ill. Be careful. I couldn't bear it if you were trapped in a marriage where your husband squandered everything we have both worked for, or treated you badly."

"Father, I promise you I will try to do as you wish, but I'm sure I shall never marry."

"You will my dear. You will." His cold, frail hand patted hers. "You wait and see. It will happen, you will fall in love, whether you mean to or not. But I know you're like your mother, you could never marry for anything but love."

An excellent father, he was never angry or fierce to her. He spoiled her a little when she was young, but with the guidance of his sensible-minded wife, they had managed to correct those character flaws early on.

For many years she was the only child, and then when she was nine, a sibling was born. She could remember it well – a cold December night. Her mother recovered well from childbirth, but another unrelated ailment struck her and she died months later. The baby, healthy at first, had caught smallpox and, although he survived, was weakened and deteriorated over the course of a year. He died in his father's arms a few months after his mother.

Louise and her father thereafter learnt to depend upon each other, and Sir Robert made sure that he passed as much knowledge on to her as he could. There was no time for frivolous learning; solid education was provided and the best tutors hired. He was never far from the classroom, and checked on her progress daily. She was a mild, receptive child, adolescence had been difficult at times; the absence of a mother meant that female companionship had to be sought through friends of her father's generation. She had been brought up almost as though she were a boy. Her indulgences had been learning those things that boys were taught: maths, history, business. But her real passion was inventions and engineering.

She did have female friends, but she found them some-what dull. Their parents didn't like their daughters to learn the things Louise did, and consequently through design and desire, most of her childhood friends were boys.

No, she regretted nothing. Finally now, she had met Jane, a young woman closer to her own age whom she felt drawn to, despite their different natures and positions. She resolved to see Jane again the next day, and knew it was unlikely that she would see Charles Lucas much, if at all. His work must keep him away from home at those times she was most likely to visit.

The next morning, Louise called on Jane and they made their way to the drapers.

"Your headache didn't last long I trust?" Jane's eyes searched her face.

"No. By the afternoon it had cleared, thankfully." Louise looked away, and hoped her countenance didn't betray her.

"I hope it wasn't caused by dining with us the night before."

"No, of course not!"

Jane lowered her head. "I thought I had offended you."

Louise stopped walking and took hold of her hand. "No! How could you ever offend anyone?"

They continued on, and arriving at the drapers, they entered to find it almost empty. Louise had never visited this particular shop before, it being not in the most fashionable part of town. But the assistant could clearly tell quality customers when he saw them and treated them with the utmost distinction and attention. They were shown an array of fabrics but both women admired the new pink silk imported from India a few days earlier.

"The colour suits you much better than me." Louise held the soft material up to Jane's face. They both turned to the small mirror on the counter.

"I do like it," Jane said. "But your dark hair matches it well too. I'm sure there are several shades of yellow and blue that I would love to wear but make me look washed out and sickly."

Louise smiled back at Jane's reflection. "If we all looked the same, it would be very boring."

They made their way home to the Lucas house to have afternoon tea and were interrupted by the unexpected arrival of Edward and Charles. Louise was secretly pleased and tried not to blush as they paid their respects to her.

"I thought you were busy today?" Jane asked them both in a petulant tone.

"We have a number of business matters to attend to here," Charles said. "We can't stay for long."

Edward interrupted, "But not so pressing that we can't stay for some tea."

It was Edward who commandeered Louise's attention at first, whilst Charles went to his study, returning after fifteen minutes with a bundle of papers and, Louise noticed ink stains on his hand.

"Miss Thomas has been telling me about her estate in Devon," Edward said to his brother. "It seems she has to return there very soon due to estate matters."

"Indeed," Charles said. "What sort of business matters do you have to deal with?"

She gave a small shrug of her shoulders. "All sorts of things. Many of the tenants request my help in overseeing repairs and helping them deal with problems, such as floods or the disposal of diseased animals. Sometimes they need advice on farming methods, and several of them are trying new ways of improving their yields. The estate has a large amount of farming machinery that the tenants borrow. It's quite interesting, although I think you would probably think it somewhat primitive compared with the projects you undertake."

She assessed his response to what she told him. He seemed interested enough, so she continued. "Unfortunately, on the odd occasion I have to intervene when they have disputes."

"Really? Disputes?" He sat down near her. "What was the last dispute you had to deal with?" It was a serious question, yet she noticed he wore a small smile. She tried to ignore how much she liked him sitting so near.

"Well," she said seriously. "The latest dispute was immediately before I came to London a week or so ago. It was between two farmers. They are brothers and they both purchased six rare breed cows; each paid half of the amount to buy the animals. One of the brothers cared for the animals whilst the other refused to help. Eventually after much protest and threats, the first brother sold the animals because he grew tired of caring for them alone. The second brother, upon hearing of the sale, demanded half of the money. But he wouldn't pay him."

"And what happened?" asked Jane, who by now was listening intently to their conversation.

"The first brother said he'd never pay him half of the

money because he didn't deserve it after all of the work he put into the animals. The animals were sold for much more than the brothers had originally paid. Eventually, a few weeks later, they asked me to resolve the issue."

"How exactly?" Charles asked.

"I spoke to both of them on their own, and heard their cases. Then, after thought and prayer for guidance and wisdom, I gave them my opinion."

"Which was?"

"That the first should pay the second a third of the money he got for the sale of the cows."

"A wise decision," Jane commented.

"A fair judgment," Edward agreed.

Charles said nothing for a few seconds, his eyes full of amusement. "It must be nice for you to get away from such petty matters when you're in London," he said eventually. She had hoped he would express his opinion of her judgment. But he was frustratingly silent on that matter.

"I do not find them petty." She shook her head and spoke in an earnest tone. "They are very important events in my tenants' lives. The two farmers I spoke of have little land, they are elderly and the cows they bought were a huge investment for them. No, I wouldn't call that petty."

He stared at her for a few moments. "Perhaps you are right. I wouldn't wish to upset you, as a guest in my house or a friend of Jane's."

He took a sip of his tea and stood up as though to go and sit with Jane, but Louise stopped him, saying, "Mr Lucas, do you not have disputes amongst your workers? You must have had some?"

"Yes. And I see what you're going to argue. You're about to compare my work to yours, and tell me that we're just the same, that we must deal with similar issues."

"But surely we both have the authority to resolve such things, and I would never dare say that any aspect of ship building, or bridge construction, or anything else is petty. The whole item cannot be built without extreme care to the details. In the same way, farming cannot be run without care to each detail, however petty it seems or however small the herd." She spoke the last words in a soft, gentle tone. If it were anyone else but him she would have put them in their place. But there was something alluring about arguing with him. She bore him no malice for having spoken what he thought. In fact, she would say anything, have any conversation with Charles Lucas, famous engineer, whatever the subject matter. But most of all she knew that he couldn't have any idea of the complexities of running an estate as large as Glazebrook, any more than she knew how to build a bridge across the Tamar.

He didn't reply, and withdrew to the fireplace to gather his thoughts. If the truth be known, to put as much space between himself and her. An engineer and a landowner; there couldn't be a greater difference. Perhaps he was biased. Of course he was. He knew he should not allow his previous dislike and experience of landowners to prejudice him, but he couldn't help it. He looked back at her – there was something about her that made him want to talk to her, made him want to believe she was different. He shook himself. What was he afraid of? That he might be attracted to her? It had been a long time since he had truly admired a woman.

A short time later, he was pleased when she approached him again.

"Mr Lucas, you and I are much the same, I feel."

He looked down at her with a smile. "How so?"

"Well, we both have many livelihoods under our care

and yet, we do not have the inclination to deal with those things that our dependents need us most for," she replied.

"You do not care to sort out the details of these people's lives?"

"If I had a choice, no. But, alas, it's my duty to do these things. I was born to it, whether I like it or not, and very often I would prefer to not have the worry of it all."

"I can't say I've ever wished to be one of my workers," he acknowledged.

"You are stern with them?"

"Not that I'm aware of. A good principal engineer must gain his men's respect and prepare to get his hands dirty helping them. It's something I do whenever I can."

"You like getting your hands dirty?" She raised her eyebrows and there was a sparkle in her eye.

"Yes I suppose I do."

His mind ran to the image of this immaculately dressed lady in front of him helping move cows, or reaping wheat. He was sure she would never help her farmers in such a way. He suppressed his amusement at the thought of her knee deep in mud and turned the conversation to something she had previously said. "But I'm surprised to hear that you lack such an inclination to care for your tenants, it's something that you have never betrayed in anything you have said before."

"What I wish for and what I have to do differ."

The brothers left shortly afterwards, leaving Jane and Louise to themselves. She was sorry he was gone, even though their conversation had been vexing at times. He seemed to blow hot and cold. Perhaps the pressure of work had left him irritable.

5

A few weeks later, Charles hurried through the drizzling rain to his offices. He took the shortest route – behind a small parade of shops to a part of town where the rent was as modest as the building itself. Most days there were a constant flow of visitors, contractors, workers, and other tradesmen, all party to the projects the partners undertook. Today, the rain seemed to be keeping them away and he entered the offices without hindrance.

The junior clerks and engineers were already at their desks, neatly organised but cramped. They acknowledged the senior partner, then went back to their work.

Charles had his own office, and some time later he was seated behind his desk writing when the door flew open. Ashton hurried in and waved a card. "Today is a day to celebrate!" he grinned.

"Why?" Charles said, not looking up until he had finished his sentence.

"Because our invitation to Miss Thomas's Engineers' Dinner has just arrived."

He handed the printed card to Charles, who studied it briefly before he handed it back.

"That is the date we were supposed to be meeting Mr Tyler about the steel order," Charles said in a nonchalant tone.

"Hang Mr Tyler. I will write to him straight away and change the date. We cannot refuse. If word got out we vetoed Miss Thomas we would never live it down. Indeed, there are several people who will be green with envy when they know we have been invited. I shall try and happen upon them accidentally as soon as I can."

Charles frowned. "Can you not go on your own?"

"Certainly not! The invitation is specific, it's you and I who are invited." He wagged his finger at his partner. "You're not getting out of this one, however much you would like to!"

"What if I were ill?"

"I'd still drag you there."

"Dead?"

"Stop it. You are going and that is final."

"But I have seen so much of Miss Thomas lately that I'm growing uncomfortable seeing her," Charles said with a sigh and sank down into his chair. "She will start to believe the only reason I speak to her is to further my reputation and work." The truth was, he couldn't stop thinking about her and wanted to keep his distance, but he was hardly going to tell that to Ashton.

"But that is precisely the reason we have this. Well, actually I think we can thank Jane for it too. You must tell her of my gratitude when you get home."

"She will not get my thanks. And I think it very improper of Miss Thomas to send out invitations so late. It's only next week. Surely she should have sent the invitations weeks ago?"

"I don't care about that! Promise me you will behave on the night of the dinner? We're fortunate to have received it, they say that there are only thirty people invited each year and that an invitation one year does not necessarily mean an invitation the next."

"Sounds very tiresome. I can't understand what all the fuss is about."

"Investors my dear boy. Investors. There will be plenty of them there, too."

"Well then, isn't it better that I do not go; I will only say something you will not like and turn the investors away."

"No you will not. Stop trying to make excuses." Ashton breathed in deeply. "If Jane stays friends with Miss Thomas, then I think we will be invited every year. You must do your best to encourage the friendship."

Charles dipped his pen in the ink and began writing again. "You'd best do that yourself. If you have finished, I have work to do," he said in a stern tone and without looking up.

When Ashton left, Charles stared at the closed door and pondered their conversation. He was annoyed by Ashton's continual praise and connivance regarding Miss Thomas and though he despised his partner's constant fawning, he knew he was doing it for the best of reasons. But the fact that he had to include him in all his plans, and expect him to perform to order was disconcerting. He was sure he would do nothing to put himself out. In fact he was determined to treat Miss Thomas the same as any other friend of Jane's; with civility and courtesy but no other special treatment. For his own sanity, at least.

Mr Ashton was incorrect in his assumption that Jane's

friendship with Louise was the reason they had received an invitation. The truth was, Louise had purposely put Charles's name at the top of the list for the dinner. She told herself that it was his skill and genius at work that put him there and that she would have added his name regardless of their recent acquaintance. But deep down she knew there was another reason. A reason she couldn't yet admit to herself.

Despite the prestige of her dinners, she was nervous that her invitation would be accepted, and she had no real doubt that he would refuse, unless business took him out of London. In the six years she had been running the dinners in her father's place, only once did someone refuse her invitation and afterwards they assured her it was because of illness.

Fortunately, she didn't have to wait long for her answer, which came the next day in the hand of Mr Ashton. She read the polite acceptance and knew how pleasant it would be to have Mr Lucas attend.

The day of the dinner arrived and she fretted over every detail. Everything was kept exactly as her father had done. How she missed him at this time of the year. She checked and re-checked every detail from the menu, the table and place settings, as well as the quality of the wine, bought from an exclusive importers. She couldn't let him down, and now years after his death, she believed she had perfected the dinners. He would be proud of her, she was sure. There were times in the past years when she wondered why she continued the tradition, but one glance at her father's portrait told her why.

There were some who frowned on what she did: a single woman hosting a group of men. She heard the whispers. She knew to some people, particularly women, it was shocking. But really, she enjoyed the company of men – especially when she was the means to bring together the great men of the age. The investors loved it too. They had a chance to meet the men who were the means of their profits. There were more reasons to continue with the dinner than not. She was sure if she didn't hold it, someone else would take over the task. Of course, it would never be as prestigious if they did.

Mr Lucas and Mr Ashton were amongst the first guests to arrive. Louise barely noticed Mr Ashton's compliments and gratitude at being amongst the lucky few, her attention, albeit covertly, was on one man. Mr Lucas bowed over her hand and greeted her formally and she noticed how smart he was in a cream waistcoat and matching cravat, a change from his usual dark ones. In his jacket pocket there was a small diamond pin and she wondered who had given it to him. Perhaps he bought it himself.

Charles Lucas wasn't one to gush, like his partner, but she discerned that he seemed pleased enough to be there, though a little awkward. She comforted herself that she was glad to have him in her house, and wore an air of happiness rarely displayed. But before their conversation could get any further, she was pulled away as more people arrived. She circulated round the guests with practiced ease, always acutely aware where he was in the room, and to whom he was speaking.

Soon enough the room was full and all the guests had arrived. Louise took a moment to cast her gaze over the room. Investors were talking with engineers. Mr Lucas wasn't far away and as a new guest, was being questioned by a number of old-timers. Louise smiled; she hoped he didn't get too many difficult questions. The conversation grew louder and for over an hour, the guests mixed. Louise made sure she spoke to everyone, excusing herself and moving to the next group with expert ease.

When dinner was served, Louise was at the head of the table, and she had placed Mr Lucas halfway down for her own sanity and presence of mind. Near to her, yet far enough away that she could concentrate on being hostess. Conversations between the gentlemen were as expected: engineering issues, and Louise noticed the usual amount of boasts displayed. Just as she had surmised, Mr Lucas wasn't one to join in with them.

Dinner was a lavish affair. Eight courses, all her own design. She had brought her cook especially from Glazebrook. Halfway through dinner, Mr Stephenson called a halt to all other conversation when he asked Louise in a booming voice, "Dear Louise, where is Mr Robert Adams this evening? You promised me he would be here tonight."

A hush settled over the table and all heads turned towards her. She placed her napkin down, looked directly back and said in a playful tone, "Why, I made no promise of the kind, as you well know. I did of course invite Mr Adams, and he accepted at first. Unfortunately, I received a note yesterday that said he had urgent business and couldn't attend after all."

"That is what you say every year," Mr Stephenson replied with a broad grin. "Yet there is no empty seat for him here at the table."

Louise closed her eyes for a moment. "I knew he wouldn't come, but if he had turned up, I would have made space for him. Besides, I cannot be responsible for Mr Adams's behaviour. If you wish to speak to him then I suggest you make an appointment."

"I have tried that, and never yet succeeded," he said.

"Aye, I have too," Mr Ashton said from further down the table. "He is very elusive. Has anyone here met him?"

There was a general murmur and shaking of heads. Nobody, it seemed had met the man.

"There," said Mr Stephenson. "None of us has ever seen him, yet everyone knows of him. Tell me, Miss Thomas, have you ever met him?"

"I suppose you could say that I have met him, yes," she said.

"Do you know him very well?" Ashton interjected in an eager voice.

"Yes, quite well."

"What sort of man is he?"

She cleared her throat. "He will be highly amused at this conversation when I tell him you are were all talking about him."

"Is anyone close to winning his flying prize?" someone asked further down the table.

Louise looked in the general direction of the man who had spoken; the elderly Mr Purnell, an investor.

"Not as far as I'm aware. I think Mr Adams eagerly awaits the time he can award his prize money."

"What prize is this?" Ashton asked.

"Mr Adams has a prize of ten thousand pounds for anyone who can invent a powered flying machine – that works." Louise said.

"It can't be done," someone murmured.

Louise spoke up in a forthright tone. "Mr Adams thinks it can be done, and I agree with him. One day, someone will invent it. Look at how far we have come in the last fifty years." Some of the men nodded, and her gaze fell briefly on Mr Lucas, to see his reaction to her words. He was listening attentively. "It may not be in our lifetime – it may not be for a hundred years, but I'm sure one day mankind will take to the skies."

"Ten thousand pounds is a lot of money," Mr Stephenson commented.

"A big incentive," someone else said.

"One thing is for sure," Mr Purnell added, "I will invest in anything Mr Adams does. He has the luck of the devil. Anyone know what his latest projects are?"

All eyes turned to Louise again. "I believe he has invested a great deal of money in the dock extensions at Bristol."

"That is Mr Lucas's project," someone said.

All eyes turned to Charles, who was in the middle of taking a sip of wine. He gave a curt nod to acknowledge the accolade.

The conversation turned to how that work was progressing and Ashton seemed particularly pleased. Louise sat back and listened to those near her with a contented smile.

When they had all moved to the drawing room after dinner, Louise was approached by Mr Stephenson.

"I hope you didn't mind my little joke at the dinner table," he said as he sipped his coffee.

"You mean regarding Mr Adams?" She dropped her voice to a whisper. "Yes, of course I minded. It was a great liberty you took and if I didn't hold such a fondness for you and your wife, I would punish you accordingly."

He laughed. "But how could I not mention Mr Adams?"

They glanced around the room. "Your choice of new blood tonight is interesting," he said, looking over to Mr Lucas.

"You disapprove?"

"Not at all. I wonder what took you so long to invite

him."

"He has only recently risen above the parapet, I believe."

"I've known him a while, and saw his potential immediately. Mr Adams may have to fight off other investors in that man now that you have identified him."

Louise shook her head. "He has nurtured his own reputation, and does not need me to further it."

"Then you underestimate your influence, dear Louise."

The evening ended after midnight and before it was over, Louise did got one more chance to speak to Mr Lucas, even though it was through coercion. Frustrated that she hadn't spoken to him – he always seemed to be in deep conversation with somebody else – she sought out Mr Ashton. She knew he would be more than willing to speak to her. She then proceeded to ask him questions about their work that only Mr Lucas could answer. Before long, Mr Ashton called over his partner. "Miss Thomas has been asking me all sorts of questions. You must speak to her so that I no longer appear stupid by not answering them."

Mr Ashton retreated.

"More questions Miss Thomas? I thought we had exhausted the subject of all my current projects," Mr Lucas said with a smile.

"Perhaps we have and I just have a bad memory," she said nervously.

Their conversation lasted just a few short minutes, before she was pulled away by guests taking their leave. But for her those few minutes were enough. He had been in her house, he sat at her table, he spoke to her of his work. The fact that he treated her no differently from her middle-aged male guests quite escaped her notice. She would have to be content with the precious little time they could spend together.

6

———

It was a rainy evening a few weeks later that Charles made his way to Perrivale's coffee house. A well established place, and frequented by many of the local businessmen, it was where Charles often met Ashton after hours to discuss business in a more relaxed atmosphere than their offices. They sometimes met with business associates, but were mostly on their own. He pushed the door open and immediately breathed in the close thick air of smoke mingled with coffee. Over in the corner at their usual table was Ashton.

He looked up over his newspaper as Charles approached. "I thought you'd be going straight home tonight."

Charles pulled out the red leather-covered chair and sat down. "Later. Mother and Jane are out visiting friends until seven."

Ashton placed his newspaper down, scrutinising Charles. "You look tired. What time did you start this morning?"

"Seven."

Ashton waved his finger. "The problem , Charles, is that you're too good, and if we're not careful you will be spreading yourself too thin. I'm more than happy to look after the investors and the cash flow, but I'm afraid you will wear yourself out and then be no good for anything or anyone. What would we do without you? I don't want to see you working yourself into the ground like Brunel."

"I can't refuse work, especially something that interests me like this new project. Besides, I do not have to be at the Tamar bridge all that often, Boyd is more than capable of looking after things."

"Yes, yes – he is very capable. But we must be careful, he lacks some experience. He doesn't have your ability to moti-vate the workers, or your insight."

"Not yet, but he'll learn. I'm sure we will not have any problem getting him to report back here in London."

"No!" scoffed Ashton.

Charles frowned. "What do you mean?"

"He is quite taken with Jane."

"He is?"

Ashton laughed at his partner. "You had no idea, did you?"

Charles shook his head.

"Hmm, too busy with work. Surely you couldn't have missed the blushes, the fluttering eyelashes and the giggles." Ashton said in a dry tone. "And that was just Boyd. Would you approve of the match?"

"There is nothing to approve of. Yet. He has made no indication to me." Charles was slightly unsettled. He thought back over the last few times Boyd had met with Jane. Why hadn't he noticed? "Are you sure there are feel-ings between them?"

"Oh yes. I think if he did decide to make his intentions known, they wouldn't be unwelcome by her."

"Really?"

Ashton laughed. "You really didn't notice, did you?"

Charles shook his head again. "It's natural I suppose. Jane is, I believe, not an unattractive woman. She is sensible too. Though part of me thinks no man would be good enough for her, but I know Boyd well enough to know he is the sort of man who would put his wife above everything else. So I suppose I can see no objections."

"You would approve of him putting his wife above the interests of our partnership and his work?"

"I would as a brother, of course. You would do well to remember that. It's what I would do too. I would always put my wife first." He added as an afterthought, "Should I ever feel compelled to marry at all, that is."

"Still no young lady can tempt you, then?" Ashton took a sip of coffee and looked at Charles with amused eyes.

"Nor you, it seems," he retorted and then continued. "No, I haven't yet met with a woman I could marry." His mind flashed to one woman but he suppressed the thought.

"And if I had a sister, I would watch over her in just the same way you do. But alas, despite my mother and father's efforts they would only have boys. I think after the sixth, mother decided enough was enough. Can't blame her really, being the only woman amongst all those men. And we were all boisterous – always fighting, always arguing." Ashton shook his head at the memories.

Charles thought of his own childhood. He and Edward had argued occasionally, but were sent to different schools, so when they saw each other during the holidays they generally got on well enough. It must have been lonely for Jane being the only child at home. She never complained of it, but she was always pleased to see them both during the holidays.

His mind turned to other matters. "Boyd is away for the foreseeable future. Besides, I wouldn't interfere in Jane's matters of the heart. I dare not." Charles thought for a moment. Jane would never make an unsuitable match. She was too careful for that. He looked across at Ashton. "We still have much business to discuss."

Ashton was about to reply, when a gentleman approached them.

"Charles? Charles Lucas? I thought it was you!"

Charles stood up and shook the man's hand. "Why, William Risinger. What a surprise! What on earth are you doing in London? I heard you were gone to France."

"I did, but I'm back," the man said.

"Permanently?"

"Possibly, but I can't say for sure."

Charles indicated that he should sit in the empty chair, and took a look at his old school friend. William Risinger was tanned and a little weather-beaten. His face was worn and lined, with deep set eyes. Was this really the same man he had known in his youth? What could have caused him to look so much older than his years?

"This is my business partner, Ashton." The men shook hands.

"How long has it been since we last met?" Charles asked.

"It must be at least two years, maybe three years at least."

"It's good to see you again, William."

"Likewise."

The two men talked for a time about Charles's work, old friends and what William was doing in London. Ashton went back to his newspaper when it became evident that Mr

Risinger wasn't well-connected, and listened in to the odd remark the pair made.

Some time later, Ashton looked at his watch. "I hate to interrupt you both, but I must be going. I'm about to try Miss Thomas to see if she will invest in a number of projects."

"Miss Thomas?" Risinger raised his eyebrows.

"Yes." Ashton sat forward, an inquisitive look on his face.

"Miss Louise Thomas from Glazebrook, Devon?"

"Yes. You know her?"

"I used to know her." His eyes shifted between Lucas and Ashton. "She used to be a friend of mine, but not any more."

"Your friendship ended? Who broke it off?"

"She did. Most adamant about it too! Told me never to darken her door again," he said with a sardonic smile.

"The friendship can't have meant much to you then – you look positively glowing that you're no longer friends." Ashton commented, then said after a pause, "Surely there must have been a reason, though?"

"I'd rather not talk of it. Rather a painful subject, but I'll tell you one day. Possibly."

Charles wasn't sure what to say. Risinger looked uncomfortable, and Charles knew him well enough not to press the issue.

Ashton was more intrigued. "Come come, you can't give us a hint of something and then not follow through. Or at least tell me what you know of her."

"I know she rarely invests in anything, so your efforts are probably in vain. She is one of those members of her class who despise the lower classes, and who think ill of the modern world."

Charles couldn't help speaking up. "That is a very different picture of her than I have noticed. She seems to be enthralled with industry and all that it entails. She has taken a great interest in my work."

Risinger was unconcerned. "Maybe she has changed since I last knew her. It has been three years."

"She has been hosting her engineering dinner for longer than that."

"Those dinners are just a tradition she has taken over from her deceased father. When I knew her, she was very good at saying one thing and doing another."

"I don't know her well enough to argue that point," Charles conceded. But he did think for a moment that Risinger must have the wrong person.

"You will have to rely on my word – as a friend. But if you know her, even a little, you will see she is somewhat different to other women."

Charles thought for a moment. "Yes, she is. I cannot presume to know women all that well, or be a great judge of them. I know her so little."

"You will have to trust me on this matter, then. I knew her when she was a child, as well as an adult. Our paths have crossed many times." He shook his head. "She can't help the way she is – her father was a selfish tyrant. Underneath, she is much the same."

"But surely, a woman who has lived so independently would appear selfish at times. She only has herself to think of."

"Of course, but it has driven her to be excessively so," Risinger said. "Now enough about that woman. Let's speak of cheerful things. How about a game of cards for a small wager? You play badly, I seem to remember."

Charles agreed, but he wondered what had taken place between his friend and Miss Thomas and whether it would make her a less suitable friend for his sister.

7

———

Louise left London for Devon a few days later, after a fond farewell to Jane and Mrs Lucas. Her estate, situated in the eastern part of Devonshire near the Axe valley, used to be a task to get to. But after the railway had opened a few years earlier, the journey became relatively quick and easy.

Her carriage was waiting for her at Axminster station. For a few years now, she had ideas for a branch line that would take passengers from Axminster, then ten miles to the sea. But there were still many locals unconvinced of its benefits.

She lowered the carriage window, and let the cool breeze in on her face as she travelled on. Her eyes searched eagerly for the landscape she had missed these last few weeks, and eventually the houses turned into trees, fields and hills. The first signs of autumn had begun here too: the leaves were a gentle brown, and a few lay scattered on the roadside. The harvest was in full swing and the fields were full of horses, carts, threshers and other new machinery. She looked forward to speaking to the farmers near her to see how the new machinery was helping them and eagerly watched those at work as she passed.

Eventually, the coach went under the ornate stone archway marking her estate's entrance and the house. She was tired and hungry, but her heart was peaceful. She was home at last.

The familiar three storey Portland stone building that dominated the landscape for miles was a welcome sight. There was only one thing that saddened her: the house would be empty. Yes, there were servants, loyal servants, but no family, and she felt her loneliness keenly at such a time as this. She should be used to it by now, but part of her still wished there was someone waiting for her to return.

As soon as she was settled in, she made her way outside and across the garden to the familiar stone barn that was now converted to her workroom. She carried with her the most recent purchases from London: a number of books and the sketch of Mr Lucas's bridge. The room smelt a little musty, but after she lit a fire, it soon warmed. She checked her miniature steam engines; they were a little dusty. She wouldn't allow the servants into this private sanctuary to clean, so she set about dusting them herself.

Afterward, she opened her new volume of chemical experiments, and picking one out, began to follow the instructions. A few hours later, she realised it was almost time for dinner, and pinning the sketch of the bridge onto the wall, she returned to her duties.

The next day, after she had dealt with a myriad of business matters with her steward and housekeeper, she called on Miss Hill, one of the local elderly ladies. She had known Louise from childhood and was always pleased to see her. The object of the visit was to meet the lady's niece, Miss Lucy Potts, who was newly arrived for a long visit. The girl was out, and Miss Hill apologised that such a distinguished visitor as herself had been let down. Louise wasn't upset, though it was inconvenient, but invited Miss Potts to call the next day at Glazebrook.

Before she left, Miss Hill entreated Louise to take the young girl under her wing, "Because her parents think her far too flighty and absent-minded at times. She needs someone to look up to who is the height of good breeding." Louise reluctantly agreed – Miss Hill had been a fount of advice and support when Louise was younger and especially when her father died. She couldn't deny her this request. Her only hope was that the niece would be pleasant company.

Niece and aunt came at the appointed time the next day and Miss Hill apologised again for at least ten minutes for Lucy being out the previous day, and explained she had been helping Mrs Barnes decorate the church for the harvest festival.

Louise took to inspecting the girl while her aunt rattled on. She was thin and petite, and she wore a straight, practiced smile upon one of the prettiest faces Louise had ever seen. Strands of blonde hair had escaped her neat bun, but Louise supposed she must have to do her hair herself. She didn't say much, her light blue eyes dancing nervously around the room. Louise wondered if Lucy had been sent to her aunt's because she was attracting the attention of too many young men. She would try and find out by asking subtle questions later.

They drank tea, then when Lucy expressed a wish to see the estate grounds, set out for a walk.

"Do you really live there?" Lucy asked when her aunt was out of earshot and they could see Glazebrook in the distance; the two of them being younger and faster on their feet.

"Yes," she answered, though she thought it an odd question.

"What, all those rooms just for yourself?"

"Yes."

"How many bedrooms are there?"

"Fifteen."

"Fifteen! I would sleep in a different one each night. Is that what you do?"

"No. I have had the very same bedchamber since I was a small girl."

"This is all so wonderful," Lucy said as they reached the end of the landscaped gardens, and walked into the outer fields. She looked around enthusiastically. "I would love to paint these scenes so that when I'm gone back home I can remember it all. I have a particular talent at painting."

"I'm sure there are many other places with equal beauty, but you may come here at any time to paint. Would you like it if we painted together?"

But Lucy's attention was already diverted by something new. "Look! There's a lake!" She pointed and ran towards it.

Louise caught her up.

"What is in the lake?" Lucy demanded, peering into it.

"What's in it?" Louise tried not to laugh. "All sorts of things. Though there are a lot of trout."

"How many fish are there?"

"I'm not sure. Although I imagine a great many."

"I would love to have my own lake!" She clutched her hands together.

"It's not that interesting surely," Louise muttered to herself. "It's only a lake."

"But if I had a lake, I would catch fish, get a boat and oh,

I don't know, do all sorts of things on it, every day. Have you got a boat?"

They continued around the water to the boathouse until Louise grew weary and decided to head back.

"Tell me about where you grew up," Louise asked as they reached the walled garden.

"It's a little place on the border in Bedfordshire; called Kensworth. Not very exciting."

"Did you enjoy growing up there?"

"Well enough. It was a little dull at times. Near London but not near enough to stay long. I'd love to see more of London, but most of all I would love to see Paris. Have you been?"

"Yes, once."

"I would love to travel to different places, see new towns, new countries, wouldn't you?"

"I can't say I've ever thought of it. Besides, I have many duties to keep me here, so really it would be impossible for me to travel any distance or for a long time."

They parted a while later and arranged to go to a fair together in a few days' time. Louise was glad to be alone after Lucy left. It wasn't that she disliked her, but the young girl talked incessantly and about so many different subjects, that Louise had hardly finished answering her first question, when Lucy asked another.

The day of the fair, Louise collected Miss Hill and Lucy in her carriage. It was a cloudy day, and in previous years it had often rained on the day of the event. Rain or no, it would take more than water from the sky to prevent the locals from attending. The event was an important one in the calendar for all and the preparations took weeks.

It was opened by the Mayor, who spoke at considerable length in a low drone and finally, to the relief of everyone, declared that the festivities should begin. The men immediately made their way to the cider tent, and the ladies to the stalls where there was produce, food and drink for sale and which numbered at least thirty. There was an array of animals on display: sheep, goats, rabbits, horses, ponies, pigs and cows, and the Falconer was centre stage. Louise's gaze swept across the familiar layout of the tents. It was the same every year, and the field was a flat one high up so that there was a full command of the valley below.

"What shall we do first?" Lucy said excitedly and looked around, completely ignoring the view.

"Whatever you like," Louise said.

"I would like to try skittles. Have you ever played?"

"Yes, many times. I have a set at Glazebrook." Lucy ran forwards. They reached them and played a few matches.

Louise won.

Lucy soon became bored, and they headed around the stalls again. When they were about to reach the metal-worker, Lucy stopped and grabbed Louise's arm, and whispered with bright eyes, "Look, there he is!"

"Who?"

"Mr Francis of course! The gentleman we spoke of the other day when we walked by the lake."

"Mr Francis? I don't recall you mentioning him, or any man."

Lucy gave a dismissive wave of her hand. "Perhaps I didn't mention him, but he was on my mind. He is stood over there!"

Louise peered over Lucy's shoulder to a group of men standing near the shire horse and cart.

"Which one is he?"

"The handsome one of course!"

Louise's shoulders dropped. "My dear, your idea of

handsome may well be very different to mine. You must give me more of an indication as to which one he is."

"He's the one stood in the middle, with the dark green waistcoat."

Louise was right, their idea of handsome was different.

"Has he seen us?" Lucy whispered.

"No, he's too busy talking with his companions."

"We must do something to attract his attention." Her wide eyes fluttered. "I long to talk to him. Although I'm not sure what I would say!" She gave a small girlish giggle.

"We're here to enjoy the fair, not talk to Mr Francis. Besides, I'm sure you will get the opportunity to speak to him today. And remember, we can hardly approach him. He must approach us."

"But I will die if I do not speak to him!"

Louise pulled her to the bee-keeper's stall and made several purchases. When she turned around to speak to Lucy, she found that she had avoided certain death and was in fact in conversation with Mr Francis.

She stood a little behind them as they talked, and wasn't close enough to hear what they said but it was clear by the blushes on both set of cheeks that the attraction was mutual. She noted that Mr Francis appeared a respectable young man: he was clean-shaven and not drinking cider; always a good sign, and he had a pleasant countenance. He looked young, probably little more than twenty-one. Just the right age for a man to fall for a pretty face.

A few moments later, Mr Francis noticed Louise waiting for Lucy and whispered something to her. Lucy turned round and made the introduction. Mr Francis spoke quickly and nervously to her, and after a few observations on the fair, Louise decided the best course of action was to end the conversation. She was only getting in their way. "Would you excuse me Mr Francis? I have a great deal of people to see today." He gave a short bow and Louise walked away saying, "Lucy, I'll see you later."

After watching these flirtations and signs of growing affection, her mind ran to a certain family in London. She had seen no outward sign that Mr Lucas liked her as Mr Francis so clearly liked Lucy, and she wondered if she ever betrayed such indications herself. She hoped not. It would be most embarrassing to blush and simper like Lucy. She must make sure it never happened. But how else was a woman to make her preference obvious?

The fair ended at four o'clock when the stalls closed, and the main marquee opened for a dance, and it seemed as though everyone was there and in good spirits too. Even the Turner brothers were sitting together and seemed to have resolved their differences, temporarily at least.

Lucy danced with many of the young men, including Mr Francis. Her beauty attracted many glances from the gentlemen, young and old. Louise danced a few times herself, having been drawn into the merriment. The lack of gentlemen didn't affect her ability to obtain a dance partner. As one of the most important people in the area she could dance with whomever she chose. During an interlude Lucy cornered Louise and demanded to know her opinion of Mr Francis.

"Do you not think him an excellent gentleman?"

"Yes, he seems very agreeable," Louise replied. "But I haven't really spoken to him, so I really can't form a proper opinion just yet."

"Then I will go and get him immediately, and you can find out everything you need to know. But I warn you – he's ever so clever and talks about all sorts of things I haven't a clue about. He's tried to teach me a few things, but I'm a hopeless student. Still, he doesn't seem to mind and keeps telling me how pretty I am. That's a good thing isn't it?"

Before Louise could stop her, Lucy marched off, and moments later returned with a somewhat confused Mr Francis. Not only that, but Lucy then walked away and left them alone.

"Miss Potts tells me you're a scholar," she asked.

"Yes ma'am."

"What subjects have you studied?

"Geology and archaeology."

"I see," Louise said eying him. He swallowed hard under her obvious scrutiny. "And do you enjoy these subjects or were you forced into studying them by your parents?"

Mr Francis's eyebrows raised in surprise. "No, I chose them myself."

"Are you an Oxford graduate?"

"Cambridge. I have recently left and I'm spending a few months with my grandparents, before I start looking for a position in earnest."

"What sort of position are you looking for? Do you wish to field study, or are you going to teach?"

"I was hoping to field study, but there are not many positions open, especially to someone with as little experience as myself."

His countenance relaxed, although Louise was by no means finished with her questions and started the onslaught again. "Well, you must start somewhere I suppose, and there must be plenty of apprenticeships. Are you taking the opportunity to study the geology and archaeology here in Devon?"

"A little, I have had the good fortune to be involved in a dig near Exeter. They think they have found a Roman villa."

"Really? How interesting. And tell me, what are the theories they are teaching on Stonehenge at Cambridge?"

They talked until Lucy claimed him for another dance. Louise had formed a good opinion of Mr Francis. He was intelligent, gentlemanly and his eyes frequently searched for Lucy as he spoke to Louise. He came from a good family line, his grandparents being well known in the area as respectable middle class. She might do far worse. So might he.

. . .

Louise saw little of Lucy for a few weeks. They were both busy in their own way; Lucy with trying to attract the attentions of Mr Francis, and Louise with the stewardship of her estate. It was on a dry Sunday afternoon after church that the two ladies met again.

Louise found Lucy alone when she called, as her aunt, Miss Hill, was visiting a friend in a nearby village for the afternoon.

"I'm so excited," Lucy told Louise before she could enter the room properly. Without waiting for her to ask why, she continued, "Mr Francis is returning tomorrow from his trip to North Devon!" She grabbed both of Louise's hands tightly.

"I had no idea he had gone away," Louise commented.

"Yes, only for a week. He was going to look at some of the cliffs or something. Anyway, he returns tomorrow."

Lucy let go of Louise's hands and they sat down.

"You still like Mr Francis then?"

"Very, very much. He calls at least three times in a week to walk out with me and has come to tea several times. Aunt Hill thinks that he may make me an offer soon." She gazed dreamily out of the window.

Louise felt a little shocked, but made sure not to show it. "Does she?"

"Yes. She said that all I need to do is encourage him as I have been and he will ask me before his six months' visit is over!"

Louise hadn't observed the two together recently, but it all felt a bit too rushed. They hardly knew each other, and he had only just begun to work; how could he possibly afford to keep a wife and the myriad of children that were bound to follow?

Louise's contemplations were interrupted after a while by Lucy's voice. "Have you ever had an offer of marriage?"

"Well, yes I have."

"What was it like?"

"It depends which one you mean. But all in all, I have received seven offers of marriage and each was very different."

"Seven!" Lucy gasped. "My goodness! And you must have refused them all, because you're not married."

"Yes, of course," Louise said, as though it were the stupidest statement ever made.

"Well, I'm not sure what I would do if I received that many offers. Were you never tempted to accept any of them?"

"Goodness me, no. Never," Louise gave a small laugh.

"I can't believe it. Seven offers. You must be excessively smug to have received that many!"

"Not at all. I found them rather exasperating really. In fact, if I were not the heir to my father's estate, I rather think I wouldn't have received any."

"Tell me about some of them, tell me about the sort of gentlemen who have asked you. I would love to know."

"Well . . ." Louise sat back in her chair. "Mr Newton: he

was such a boring man I fell asleep every time he started to speak. Even when he was proposing I didn't realise it. It was only when he was on one knee that I suddenly asked him what he was doing down there and I had to ask him to repeat what he had said! He didn't seem to mind me asking him to repeat himself, but was rather upset when I refused him.

"Then there was Mr Bulford. He was far too old; older than my own father – I couldn't have married him!" She shook her head. "I couldn't understand why he made me the offer in the first place. He had a large estate of his own, so he couldn't have been after Glazebrook. It wasn't until about six months later I heard a report that he had had to sell his own estate and was living in a small house in Bath with only two servants! Anyway, he was only after my inheritance.

"Then there was Mr Lee. I had only known him a week. He was handsome and charming, but far too reckless. Father would never have approved."

"Weren't you the smallest bit tempted?"

"Oh Lord no! Certainly not. He was a gambler."

Lucy opened her mouth and was about to speak, but was stopped by Louise as she continued on.

"Then there was Mr Dupont. He was one of my tutors. Frenchman. I was only fifteen when he proposed. As soon as I told father, he sent him away that instant. Father wouldn't let the poor man pack his clothes. He was escorted off the estate and onto a train and his belongings were sent on afterwards. He wrote to me a few weeks later telling me how much he loved me, but again, after I showed the letter to father, I never received another one. I would like to know what father did to stop him writing again, but alas he never did tell me."

Louise gazed out of the window. She rather wondered

why, if Mr Dupont had loved her, he hadn't contacted her after her father's death. She really did wonder what had happened to the man. Perhaps it was better not to know.

"Then there was Mr Gaffney. My goodness, I cannot but help laughing when I think of him!" It was a few moments before she could control her laughter.

"Whatever did he do that was so amusing?"

"Well," Louise said, stifling giggles. "He proposed to me the first time he met me. It was at an assembly in London. Horrible place, the music was dreadful, the refreshments were dire and there were too many drunken men and it was so hot! I was there with my cousin, Lord Philip, and a few other acquaintances. It was Philip's idea to go. He seems to like these things. After I had been introduced to Mr Gaffney he cornered me near the refreshments and proposed there and then!"

"My goodness, that is rather odd. Why ever did he propose so quickly?"

"For my inheritance, of course. I tried not to laugh at him, even if he was blatantly mercenary."

"So it wasn't love at first sight then?"

"Certainly not. He was obnoxious. Thought he would be doing me the favour by marrying me. The impudence of it."

They sat for a while in silent contemplation.

"Father always used to tell me I could marry any man I chose," Louise remarked after some time.

"What? Any man?"

"Well those who were not married already!" Her face grew more serious, and she placed her teacup down. "He used to tell me that I was lucky to be able to choose and that most women had to accept whoever made them an offer, whatever their sentiments."

"I hope I won't have to do that," Lucy said, with a sad look in her eye.

"I'm sure you won't my dear. I'm sure you won't. You have so many excellent qualities that Mr Francis will have to stand behind all the other gentlemen who will ask for your hand."

"But don't you find it difficult to know if a gentleman loves you and doesn't want to marry you for the money?"

"It's the primary concern to me whenever I meet a gentleman for the first time. But you know there are plenty of them who are wealthier than me. They'd better watch out!"

Lucy looked unsure whether to take Louise seriously. "I would have thought that the ideal husband for you would be someone who didn't know you were rich or owned an estate. He would love you without knowing about it." She looked pleased at her analysis. "You could pretend to be poor and when a gentleman falls in love with you you'll know for sure that he wants you and not the money! Or better still, so that you do not have to pretend to be someone else, a gentleman who wasn't interested in your inheritance at all. But is there such a man?"

"I'm sure there is somewhere," Louise said. The conversation was starting to be a revelation to her. There was one man who seemed uninterested in her estate. She pushed him from her mind for what seemed like the hundredth time that day.

"Do you think a gentleman could possibly not be interested in my money?" Louise asked. But it was more a question to herself. For what would a nineteen-year-old girl know of it?

A gentleman who wasn't interested in my inheritance.

The words hung over her. She knew Mr Lucas enough to

realise that his heart and soul lay in his work, in his bridge designs, his tunnels and his other engineering feats. This was the age of engineering and he was at the centre of it. What interest would he have in a country estate?

She no longer made herself push the thought of him aside as she had been desperately doing since she returned to Devon. She allowed her mind to linger on all she knew of him, both from her own experience and from what she knew of his dealings with Robert Adams.

He was handsome – to her at least. Not classically so, but she never did find ordinary looks appealing. He cared for his sister and mother in a most attentive way. Jane had revealed that he often worked long hours and therefore certain weeks she didn't see him much. But when he was at home, he was always the kindest, most thoughtful brother. If she wanted justification for her growing adoration then this only fueled it.

To break from these ruminations she suddenly said, "Lucy, you must not get your hopes up with Mr Francis."

Lucy looked up at her, her blue eyes wide with longing. She quickly added, "What I mean is, you must remember that a man like Mr Francis must have employment before he could take a wife."

"I see what you mean," Lucy said, with a note of sadness in her voice.

Louise took hold of her hand. "But I'm sure that once he has these prospects, he will not hesitate to secure your affections. Besides, he may propose and you will have to be engaged until he has such a position. I have known several couples come to an understanding even though material circumstances have been against them for some time."

"I hope he finds something soon."

"I'm sure he will, I'm sure he will."

8

————

It was a few weeks since Charles had met with William Risinger that first time, and though they had met a number of times since, Charles had forgotten his promise to himself to find out the circumstances behind the breakdown of Miss Thomas's friendship with his friend. The everyday stresses and pressure of his work pushed all such thoughts from his mind and it wasn't in his nature to linger on trivial matters. But his curiosity was roused once more when he saw Risinger sitting in a large comfortable chair near the window one evening at Perrivale's coffee house.

Risinger looked up and cast aside his newspaper. "Charles!" he stood up and shook his hand. "Won't you join me?"

Charles sat down.

"If I look a little more tired than usual," Risinger said. "It's because I have been making arrangements. I'm emigrating to America."

Charles's eyebrow's rose. "Really? When do you leave?"

"Well, I thought I may go in about six months. I have

some personal matters to take care of and friends to take leave of. I think once I'm gone I shall never return," he said with a sigh.

"You do not wish to go?"

"Well, there is not much for me here in England." He paused for a moment. "Certain people have made sure that I do not have many prospects here."

"Really? Who?" Charles sat forward.

Risinger looked away for a brief moment, as though deciding whether or not to say anything. His mouth formed the words, "Miss Louise Thomas." He paused after he said the words and then in a louder voice asked, "Do you know if she is in London at the moment?"

Charles frowned. "No, I don't think she is. Why do you ask?"

"Only that since I'm not her most popular person I would very much like to stay out of her way."

"Surely it cannot be that bad?"

"It's more me than her. Things might get a bit heated if we met and I'd tell her exactly what I thought of her."

Charles was about to ask what the problem was when they were interrupted by one of the waiters, who approached to tell Mr Lucas that his sister was waiting for him outside.

"Well then, Risinger, you must come and meet my sister Jane. I'm sure you will like her."

Risinger smiled. "Of course, it would be an honour."

They both made their way out of the coffee house to find Jane standing just outside. The introduction was made and Charles noticed that Risinger seemed as affable as ever. He had an easy way of conversing with people, but especially with women.

"What do you think of Mr Risinger?" her brother asked once they parted.

"He seemed a pleasant enough man," Jane said nonchalantly, but she offered no further comment.

"Is that all you have to say?" He glanced at her face to try and read her expression.

"Yes. I don't remember him much, but I think I will have to meet him a little more if I'm to give you an informed opinion. But straight away I could tell he was a ladies' man."

Charles burst out laughing.

"What is so amusing?"

"Risinger, a ladies' man? At school he was always the biggest oaf with girls. Not that we met many."

"People change, Charles. And he seemed to be the kind of man who was used to putting an act on in front of a woman." She grabbed his arm. "Forgive me, I don't mean to be mean about a friend of yours. But you always like honesty. I will endeavour to like him."

Charles contented himself with that.

. . .

It was a few months later, in March, when Louise returned to London. Many of her friends would be in town, but there was one family in particular which drew her. She spent the time leading up to her visit giving in to those feelings that she tried to drive away and now, one last attempt was to be made. She was determined to see Mr Lucas again and let her heart decide if what she felt was love or simply a passing fancy. She had little to compare her feelings to, because she had never felt herself to be in love before. During her time away she was in constant correspondence with Jane, and had been called upon to explain her continued absence from London more than once.

She left behind a distraught Lucy. The girl hadn't received an offer from Mr Francis and he had left Devon a few days before. Louise was rather relieved to go to town because she didn't know if she could cope with her friend's anguish any longer. Lucy had turned up at Glazebrook several times in tears and asked for advice. Louise, although sympathetic, grew weary. She wasn't the best person to ask about such matters and did not have inclination to tend to a young broken heart. Generally though, when she wasn't thinking about Mr Francis, Lucy was improving in maturity. Louise discovered the girl had a talent not only for painting, but for writing poetry, and the two had spent many an afternoon discussing the latest works.

Lucy had to content herself with the thought that Mr Francis had promised to write to her, although Louise wasn't so optimistic. Mr Francis was a young man with no ties and who needed employment. She knew it was unlikely he would find time to write or that he would be inclined to do so. She didn't mention her doubts to Lucy.

So, Louise sat happily with Jane in London. They sipped tea, and talked over the last few days. Both ladies enjoyed being back in each other's company even during those moments when they had nothing to say. Louise hadn't seen Mr Lucas yet and eagerly anticipated a meeting. She would know the instant she saw him if her heart had been won over as she believed.

"When did you say your mother would return from Bath?" Louise asked.

"Next week. Have you ever been?"

"Yes, a few times. I have taken the water too; such an odd taste! I can't say it did me any good, but then I was lucky not to have any ailment at the time."

They were interrupted by the sound of someone approaching. The door opened and Charles entered. The moment she had been waiting for had arrived. He greeted Louise with a small bow. She knew the instant she saw him.

She loved him.

She barely knew him, and she had only spoken three words to him for months, but she knew it the instant she laid eyes on him.

While these revelations pulsed through her, Louise barely noticed that another man had entered the room behind. Louise looked up to greet the man, paused, then withdrew her outstretched hand.

It took a moment for Louise and Mr Risinger to realise they were in each other's company. Their eyes met and then instantly looked away. Louise clutched the arm of the chair, uncertain what to do.

Risinger swallowed hard, then turned away and looked out of the window.

Apparently oblivious, Jane stood and rang the bell for more tea, but unable to bear being in the same room as William Risinger, Louise stood up and hurried out of the room.

Jane, having seen her leave, followed her into the hallway.

She put her arm around her. "Are you unwell?"

"Yes. No. I – er. I feel ill and I must leave immediately. Would you be so good as to call me a cab?" She placed her arm against the wall for support. Her face felt hot and she felt nauseous.

"Of course," Jane said sympathetically. "Will you not come into the study and sit quietly while I arrange it? I will take you there." It was a command more than a question and Louise didn't argue. Jane took her arm and led her the short distance to the study and seated her in one of the lounge chairs near the fireplace.

Jane left the room and Louise panicked for a moment. What if Risinger came in? The few minutes before Jane returned felt like hours. When she did, she was holding both their bonnets and cloaks.

"Come my dear, the cab is waiting."

Jane led her outside. The short journey was over quickly and Jane tended to her friend when they reached her home. Louise's maid indicated those home comforts that she found advantageous. Jane left half an hour later, after Louise insisted that she was feeling better and would prefer to sleep for a while.

When Jane returned, she found Charles alone.

"How was Miss Thomas?" he asked with a distinct note of disgust in his voice.

"A little improved. I cannot say what ailed her, but I think she will be better shortly."

Jane gazed at her brother. His scowl betrayed a certain amount of anger that had brewed for the last few hours.

"I should sooner have worried about Mr Risinger. He was shocked that Miss Thomas was here."

"Why?" Jane asked. "She is my friend. Why should she not be here?"

Charles then explained that he knew about Mr Risinger and Miss Thomas's broken friendship.

"I don't know the circumstances that led to the breakdown of the friendship yet," he explained. "But I do know that he was shocked to see her and that he was unhappy she now knows he is in the country."

Jane shook her head. "I don't know what to think. Louise is my friend, and I've only met Mr Risinger a few times, despite your previous friendship with him."

"He was a fellow student at school."

"But what could Mr Risinger possibly fear from Louise?

She is such a kind-hearted and generous lady, I cannot believe that any man would fear her. She is just a woman."

"She is a woman with great wealth and influence," Charles said. "And although I do not know all of the details, William has told me that he is unable to get work because of her interference. He is emigrating because America is the only place with opportunities where Miss Thomas cannot touch him."

They stood silent for a moment. "I do not believe she is capable of such a thing,' Jane said. 'I believe we both should not jump to conclusions. But why would Miss Thomas leave so suddenly and appear so ill at the sight of Mr Risinger if she wields so much power over him?"

It was an interesting point, but after a moment he had his answer. "A woman in her position does not have to do the work of influence herself. She will have paid men to ensure that Mr Risinger does not gain work. Therefore, seeing the man himself on her own must have been a shock."

"If what you say is true, then my friend must have a good reason. Have you not thought of that? You must not be so one-sided until you have found out all the facts. He could have harmed her."

"Whatever the reason, I'm determined to find out everything now." He softened a little. "You're right Jane. I must find out the whole truth."

. . .

At home, a thousand thoughts swam in Louise's mind. Risinger back in England? He had been the very last person she had expected to see – and in the Lucas house too. She felt sick at seeing him. But she was also angry at herself for reacting the way she did. How could she be so weak? She told herself that if she ever saw him again she would be strong. He looked different, older, withered. But underneath the cool exterior, he was still the same man. She could see it in his eyes. One question bore onto her: how did Risinger and Mr Lucas know each other? She scolded herself for not having asked Jane. She thought it strange that Risinger was friends with Charles Lucas, the brother of her new friend. This seemed to be no coincidence. and she feared what the consequences might be. She knew she had to act and act quickly. She wrote to her lawyer, Mr Russell.

After the shock of seeing Risinger had subsided, Louise allowed her thoughts to stray in another direction. She was disappointed not to have spoken to or seen more of Mr Lucas. The few moments she saw him didn't give her the time to gauge his feelings, even if she now knew her own. It was inconvenient.

Jane called the next day and enquired after her. Louise saw her briefly, so that she was assured of her recovery. They arranged to meet the next day to visit a gallery but before she left, Louise asked Jane how long her brother had known Mr Risinger.

"They were at school together. But they have only met a few times in the last few months," Jane explained.

"Are they close friends?"

"Not at all. Charles said he only knew Mr Risinger a little at school, and like I said, they have only met a few times since they met again recently."

"Your brother – he is not a man who is dazzled by wealth, or who seeks it, I think?"

"Charles? No not at all. As you may be aware, his interests lie solely with engineering feats. In fact, sometimes I find him exasperating, he is so single-minded."

"Yes, that is what I thought. Tell me one more thing. His

reputation as an engineer is impeccable; is he always honest and true?"

Jane frowned, "Have you heard something that taints his character?"

"No, no. Not at all. I'm sorry, it is an impertinent question and I shouldn't have asked it."

They sat in awkward silence for a moment until Jane said, "Charles has always had the highest morals. He never was and never has been a man to wilfully do anything wrong."

Louise took hold of Jane's hand. "That is exactly what I thought."

When Jane arrived home, Charles was waiting for her in the sitting room.

"Well? What excuse did Miss Thomas give for her behaviour yesterday?" he demanded.

"Excuse? Why would she need an excuse? She asked how you and Mr Risinger knew each other, so I told her the truth – that you were at school together and had met again recently."

"Is that all?"

"Yes, and I'm tired of this subject. Haven't you got a tunnel to design? Or something else to keep you occupied."

"I have enough work, as you well know."

"Then I can't see why you're so interested. It's so unlike you to be concerned with personal matters."

"Risinger is my friend."

"Why are you so determined to dislike Miss Thomas? What has she done to you that places her so low in your opinion?"

"Nothing. She has done nothing to me. I suppose it's more what she represents than who she is. I do not know the circumstances of her dealings with Mr Risinger, but I do not like her obvious interference in his affairs. It's officious."

"Neither of us knows the truth. It seems they dislike each other, but without knowing the details, we can't make an informed judgment."

"That is true, but if she is anything like the gentry I have been at the mercy of many times during my work, she will be the one at fault."

"How can you say that? You seem happy to classify her amongst the worst of her class, when she could be the best."

"From what I have been told, she is not among the best."

"Told by Risinger?"

"Yes."

"Why should you believe him above anyone else?"

"He is a gentleman. He is an old school friend. Why would I not believe him? What possible reason could he have to slight Miss Thomas?"

"I don't know. But, come Charles, we must not argue! Especially over something so wholly unconcerned with us." Jane put her hand on her brother's arm and he patted it then stood up.

"I suppose so. I'm going to the study to work." He was determined to keep the peace and retreated to his private sanctuary.

. . .

Louise and Jane attended the gallery the next morning to find a small amount of rain didn't spoil their plans, but cleansed the air somewhat and made their journey as pleasant as could be expected on a warm March day in London.

It was after their visit to the gallery was over and they had walked home that Louise decided to speak her thoughts.

"I'm glad to be able to spend time with you again Jane. Your friendship is important to me. I hope you realise that."

Jane stopped and looked at her friend. "It's important to me too. I hadn't realised until you left for Devon all those months ago. I hope you can stay longer in London this time."

"I hope so too, but I would be honoured if you and your mother would be my guests at Glazebrook sometime in the near future. I would very much like to have you stay."

"I would like that very much too. Tell me – how long does it take to travel to the Tamar from your estate?"

"I'm not entirely sure, but I would have thought about half a day. There is a train that will take you as far as Plymouth. Why do you ask? You want to see how your brother's bridge is progressing?"

"Yes," Jane answered hesitantly. "Actually, there is someone I would like to see if I were to visit Devon. He is a good friend."

"He?" Louise said, with amusement in her eyes.

Jane blushed a little. "Yes, he."

"And is he involved with the building of the bridge?"

"Yes. He is there all the time overseeing everything. He is the principal engineer."

"And you would like to see him again?"

"Very much."

"I can relate to such feelings myself. You need not be embarrassed."

"You can?" Jane looked into Louise's face and wondered who could have made her feel such things. Mr Risinger? Was that the reason for her reaction the other day?

"What is the gentleman's name in Devon?"

"Henry Boyd. But you must not say anything to anyone. Promise me, please."

"Of course. You have my word. But why the secrecy?"

"Well, it's that I'm not sure if he truly returns my senti-ments. I would be rather embarrassed if he didn't and I wouldn't want him to feel under any obligation because he works for Charles."

"Have you thought about writing to him?" Louise asked, thinking of her new friend Lucy Potts.

"He has written to me a few times and I have written back. But he was formal in his letters and gave nothing away. It was all rather vexing."

"I see your point. Why write at all if you're going to be only formal?"

"Exactly. I did wonder whether he held back because he was unsure of my feelings. I believe that I made them clear enough. I'm not one to hide such things."

"Well, I do not think it a good idea that you write to him explicitly about your sentiments; that wouldn't be seen to be right. It's difficult for women, isn't it? But I wonder, could you not let your brother know of your feelings. Perhaps if he thinks Mr Boyd a suitable match, he could relay your senti-ments to him?"

"I'm not sure. I think Charles knows, although I have never spoken to him about it. I'm certain Mr Boyd has said nothing about me, especially to his employer," Jane said.

"It's a puzzle to know what to do. I do sometimes dislike the fact that a lady should not make her sentiments known to a gentleman. But we will have to bear it as best we can. Has he given you an indication of his feelings?" Louise asked.

"He certainly is most attentive when we meet, though when Charles is near he does seem a little reserved at times, which is most of the time. Mother is very good and tries to look for opportunities to pull Charles away."

Louise smiled and inclined her head in understanding.

"Enough about me," Jane said. "Now tell me, you said you knew how I felt. Who is the gentleman you admire?"

Louise tried not to blush, and turned away. Her gaze fell on the buildings around them, the trees, the street. Anything except his sister's face. "Oh, it's nobody. But alas, I have no mother or brother to help me along. So I shall have to do it myself!"

Jane didn't press the issue further, though she was more than curious to find out who had managed to secure her friend's affections.

A few days later and the friends found themselves together at a local assembly. It was somewhere the Lucases attended occasionally when the weather was bad, or when evening entertainment at home grew a little wearisome. Mrs Lucas was in attendance, having returned from her trip to Bath, and was pleased to see Louise, and their friends the Hunters. Louise had yet to speak to Charles or see him since that day Risinger had shown up. She was disappointed to hear that he wasn't to attend the assembly, but resolved not to let the evening be dampened by the news. As always, she dressed with the utmost care: a green silk gown – one of her finest.

"Charles has to work late again, he sent word this afternoon, but Jane and I were determined to attend tonight," explained Mrs Lucas when they were all gathered. Edward escorted the party and seemed rather more jovial than Louise remembered. His wife Rose was as friendly as ever and introduced her to many of their friends. It seemed she knew half the room.

It was some time into the evening, while standing near the entrance, and regaining her composure after a lively dance, that Louise noticed a familiar figure enter the room.

It was Charles Lucas. She didn't expect him, but her heart was filled with gladness and expectation. Finally she hoped to speak to him freely. From her position in the room she could observe him without being seen herself. He stood tall and with self-confidence, perfectly groomed, she couldn't tear her gaze from him. She watched as he entered, looked around and upon seeing his sister, mother and Miss Hunter, walked over to them. Their delight at seeing him was obvious and Louise noted a small blush on the cheeks of Miss Hunter as she greeted him with a flutter of lashes. Louise was instantly jealous, though not surprised that another woman would be attracted to him. Still, she couldn't help thinking Miss Hunter was a poor insignificant. She was a nobody compared to herself. Miss Hunter's fortune was one thousand pounds. Louise laughed inwardly. One thousand! Her inheritance was at least one hundred times that. She quickly tried to calculate how much it was all worth. It was impossible.

Despite these thoughts, Louise suddenly felt overcome with a nervousness she had seldom felt before. The feeling unsettled her. She had been about to return to Jane, but now that her brother was there she had a strange self-consciousness about doing it and remained where she was.

So, for fifteen minutes, she stood on her own. She watched the assembly – or at least appeared to. For she saw the people dance and talk, but her thoughts were far away at the other end of the room.

She knew the moment he walked in the room that her heart was his for the taking. She had known it for months. But now, on seeing him again, she surrendered a part of her never yielded before.

If she had been capable of thinking of anyone else other than herself and the object of her affection, she would have felt a great deal of empathy for Lucy Potts and her Mr Francis, whose circumstances meant their match would be unlikely for some time. Not so for her. For what was there that could possibly prevent her marriage other than either party's own approval or disapproval? Eventually she realised that, if she didn't do something and move from her spot, what was left of the evening would be wasted; her on one side of the room, him on the other.

It was Jane who ended the stalemate. She saw Louise on her own in her miserable solitude. She whispered a quick "be nice to my friend" to her brother and went to collect her.

Charles did as his sister asked, and greeted Louise with cordiality. She tried not to blush in the same way as Miss Hunter.

"It's a surprise to have you here, Mr Lucas. Jane said you were too busy with work."

"I was. But I grew exasperated with a pressing issue and decided to come home only to find that my entire family were out enjoying themselves." He turned a little away from her, as though to exclude her from any further conversation.

Louise didn't notice, or wouldn't let him escape. "I have always found if work was taxing, an evening such as this can provide an adequate amount of respite."

She had rather hoped that he would ask her to dance, for the next was about to begin. But this wasn't to happen. He was cruelly pulled away from her by his elder brother to speak with a friend.

His mother took his place and said in a quiet voice to her whilst they looked at the dancers, "Charles seemed pleased to see you again."

Louise immediately stared at her to see if she was in earnest. It appeared so. Her heart leapt.

"Do you think so? I think he was equally pleased to see Miss Hunter. I rather think she holds an affection for him."

Mrs Lucas gave a tight smile. "Well, if she were – that would be hard luck for her. His family could never approve of her as a match. Not when there is a more – if you understand me . . ." she paused and tried to find the right words, "A more worthy and consequential lady in his acquaintance of whom we approve in every way." To add weight to her words she took hold of Louise's hand and patted it.

Louise met her gaze. "I understand you completely."

"I'm glad we comprehend one another on this matter."

It took Louise a few minutes to fully absorb the conversation. She felt a swell in her heart that she met with his family's approval. But at the same time was a little mortified that her feelings were obvious. Then she remembered the conversation with Jane when she had told her that she had made her sentiments for Mr Boyd plain. Perhaps it was for the best. For how else would he know of her feelings? She had learnt from an early age that most gentlemen were a little slow reading the signals from a woman. But now with his mother forwarding the match, she hoped that a happy conclusion was inevitable. She couldn't bear the thought of any other outcome.

She left that evening without speaking any more to Mr Lucas. But she was certain that, given a little more time, things would come to their natural conclusion. She had to be patient.

9

A few days later, Charles stood outside William Risinger's lodgings and rang the bell. A young servant boy answered and he was shown through. Risinger's room, one of about eight in the same building, was a little shabby, but respectable. It was oddly stark – but since there were no pictures on the walls, it was no surprise. There was a sweet tobacco smell wafting through; one he had come across before, but he couldn't remember where. He stepped around a number of wooden crates scattered on the floor, some half-filled with objects neatly packed in newspaper.

"Charles!" Risinger extended his arm and the two shook hands. "Now, what have you come to see me about? I can see purpose in your visit."

"You're leaving so soon? I thought you were not going for at least six months."

"Indeed, I have received my marching orders from Miss Thomas and alas I must go by Wednesday next week." His voice was jovial, but his countenance betrayed a large amount of indignation.

"She has told you to leave?"

"Yes. And I must go." He surveyed the room, a mournful look in his eye.

"But surely you do not have to leave because of her? You cannot relinquish yourself?"

"I do and I must. She has too much influence." he shook his head.

"How can you let her triumph over you?"

"Yes, 'triumph'. That is an excellent description for it. You may think me weak, but a man in my position has little choice other than do what I'm bid by those with the money and power. She has made sure I have no other option than to leave."

"Is there anything I can do to help you? I have little influence but I will gladly help in any way in my power."

"I don't think so. I shall go earlier to America and I will prosper there, I'm sure," he said with a forced smile.

"William, tell me why Miss Thomas treats you so? I would like to know. My sister is friends with her. Is she in danger? I would like to know for her sake."

Risinger shook his head. "I will say, but I would rather you didn't go about telling everyone. I'm rather embarrassed, really."

"You can be assured as a gentleman that I would never go about telling anyone your business."

Risinger indicated that they should sit down. They did so in the armchairs by a small fireplace, where a single pitiful log had burnt itself out.

"Where shall I start?" Risinger said. "I suppose with her father, Sir Robert. He was a good friend of my own dear father. The two knew each other from childhood; my father moved to Devon to a nearby village when he was twelve. My father was summoned to be a playmate for Sir Robert. This is a common occurrence, you may know that already. They paid his family well and at least he received the same education as Sir Robert and they stayed friends for their entire lives. My own father married and two years later I was born. Sir Robert was naturally my godfather.

"I saw little of Sir Robert through my childhood; we moved to Exeter when I was a baby and he was too busy with his own matters to bother to see me. But occasionally when we would all visit him he seemed pleasant enough. When Sir Robert died, I had just started at Cambridge. Miss Thomas visited me there, and I was pleased to get to know her. As a child a little younger than me, she was singular and distant, but she seemed to have cast off these childhood eccentricities and was civil and attentive. But I did notice sometimes how spoilt and selfish she was.

"Through her own insistence we became friends and her visits became more frequent. She asked me to visit her in Devon many times. I couldn't always go but went when I could. On one such visit, I discovered something about her which, well . . ." He paused and raked his hand through his hair.

"The second night of my visit, there was a storm. I've never been one to sleep through such noise, and it kept me awake for a long time. I was restless and made my way to the kitchens in order to get refreshment. I didn't want to disturb the servants, they were worked so hard and paid so little I felt sorry for them. I returned to my chamber, and was about to close the door when I heard talking and laughing. I looked out into the hallway and by the moonlight coming in through a great window I saw Miss Thomas and a man embracing in the doorway of her chamber. They didn't see me. I was shocked. Surprised. But my bewilderment was surpassed when the next day I saw the man in question was one of the grooms."

Charles let out a deep sigh and closed his eyes for a short time.

Risinger continued, "You may well sigh like that Charles. It became clear after a few days that Miss Thomas had frequent visitors to her bedchamber. Why would a woman of her wealth and power marry? She would no longer be mistress of her estate or of her life. Instead, this way she could retain her position and her night-time visitors could attend to her other needs. It wasn't until a few months later I visited Devon again that one night my worst fear was realised."

"What happened?"

"For some time I saw her watching me when she thought I didn't notice. She became over friendly with me. Taking hold of my hands and not letting go for a long time. That sort of thing. One night she drank a little more wine than normal and propositioned me. She demanded that I visit her bedchamber. I couldn't. I have high moral standards, of course. It would go against everything I was ever taught, or believe in, even if I were attracted to her. She is, after all, a very beautiful woman."

Charles had listened quietly but couldn't hold back any longer. "It's amazing to me how she manages to convey such maidenly graces, when she holds such carnal knowledge and behaves in such an immoral way." He thought back to the last time he had seen her at the Assembly. While she was laughing and dancing, her lackeys were ordering his friend out of the country. He felt his heart quicken in anger.

"Yes, but I suppose she lies even to herself. When she propositioned me it was like . . ." he paused again to find the right words, "It was like she was another woman, a different woman; as if she were possessed. I'm not sure if it was the wine or not."

"What happened then? When you refused, I mean?"

"She was angry. Told me if I didn't do as she wished then she would make me pay. I didn't believe she meant it, especially with the amount of wine she had drunk. I thought she would forget about it the following morning."

"And did she?"

"No. She gave me one last chance. But I refused again."

Risinger stood up, went to the window and looked out.

"She ordered me off her estate and her last words to me – I shall never forget – she said, "You will live to regret your decision forever, Mr Risinger." I haven't regretted it but she has made my life extraordinarily difficult."

He remained at the window. After a while, Charles said, "Thank you for telling me. I'm shocked, but your disclosure has confirmed my worst suspicions about her. I had already noticed that she speaks and acts in a most unladylike manner sometimes. It's almost as though the mask slips on occasion."

Risinger turned around. "I knew you were a perceptive man. There is one more thing you should know. Miss Thomas has not had so many lovers for such a long time without consequences of her actions."

"Do you mean . . . ?"

"Yes, she has a child, a daughter," he said. "It was a few years ago. She does not look after or acknowledge the child herself, of course; it's being brought up by a family in a village near her estate. A childless couple."

"But who is the father? Why doesn't she look after the child? Surely she should at least support it, even if she does not acknowledge it."

"I do not believe she knows who the father is. It could be one of many men I suppose."

"How did you learn of this?"

"It was by chance, actually. A few months after I was seen off the Glazebrook estate I ran into a former footman of hers in London. He told me. He said he left her service because she made demands on him, and he a happily married man who was devoted to his wife. It seems no man is safe around her. I can assure you though, I looked into what this man told me. I tried to obtain proof of the adoption, but it seems Miss Thomas has paid off many people in order to hide her mistake. They would all speak to me in private, and confirmed it; but officially, they would admit nothing."

Charles stayed silent. It was too much to take in. This woman (he couldn't call her a lady now) had fooled him. On the outside she was all modesty, charm and affability. But he knew the truth. He scolded himself; he was the one who had introduced her to his sister. It was most regrettable.

"I see what you're thinking. You cannot believe that a lady could abuse her position so; could behave in such an unseemly and immoral way."

"I find it all incomprehensible. But I do not understand why you find it embarrassing. You have followed your principles – you always did when we were at school. You were the perfect pupil. Everyone said it."

"Thank you Charles, your kind words are gratefully received. Many gentlemen who might find themselves in the same position wouldn't have chosen the moral path I have. Indeed, if I had given into her, I'm sure she would have adorned me with gifts and money until she grew tired of me, then I would be in a much better position than I'm in now."

"You honour yourself by not giving in to her."

Risinger gave a small tip of his head. "Thank you. I always try to do the right thing."

Charles didn't stay much longer. They agreed to meet one more time before Mr Risinger was to travel to Liverpool. Charles decided that he must take immediate action. He wasn't going to allow his sister's reputation to be sullied by Miss Thomas. He must put a stop to their friendship without delay. He would also demand that Miss Thomas relinquish her stranglehold on his friend.

He decided to go straight to see her and concluded that there was no reason to delay, even though the hour was late. But unfortunately when he called, she wasn't at home, having gone out for the evening.

Overnight, he didn't lose his determination and called again mid-morning. Again, she was out and he started to wonder if she was ever at home.

. . .

When she arrived home from a day visiting friends, Louise was pleased to hear that Mr Lucas had called that morning as well as the night before, although she was a little dismayed that she had been out both times. It was unfortunate luck. She was told he would return later that afternoon in the hope that she would speak with him. Her heart murmured the reason why he had called on her, and although things were moving faster than she expected, there wasn't a doubt now in her mind that this was what she wanted. He obviously wanted to see her; calling twice within such a short period of time wasn't to be sniffed at.

A thrill went through her. She tried to remember the times she had watched in amusement all the other women at balls, at social events and such, where they flirted and tried to gain the attentions of the one gentleman they admired. She tried to remember the small encouragements they gave to the men. What subtleties did she need to perform to show this man that any special notice he showed her was welcome and that his addresses to her would be accepted?

It was a new sensation. She liked it. Succumbing to her feelings – giving into them – was delicious. She felt free, unrestrained, for the first time a real woman.

Perhaps his mother had spoken to him with discretion, dropping hints that she was willing to receive and accept his affections. She would soon find out, because as she stood near the window on the second floor, she heard the bell and hurried herself to the drawing room to receive him.

10

───────

The servant announced Mr Lucas, and Louise curtsied her welcome. He in turn gave a curt bow and they both waited for the door to close before either spoke.

She began in an eager voice and to fill the awkward silence. "Mr Lucas, I'm very pleased to see you," she said, stepping forward a little. He seemed surprised and took a step back, but there was no further escape, he was right by the door.

"Will you not sit down?" she indicated to the sofa he was near.

He sat at one end, but remained silent. All he could hear was the loud tick of the clock.

He glanced at her; she was watching him closely with a look of expectation.

Charles suddenly felt foolish. Miss Thomas looked perfectly respectable: a soft smile on her face, dressed in cream muslin. Despite his reason for being there and his knowledge of the truth, he thought her becoming all the same. But he wouldn't let her beauty detract from the task.

Eventually he muddled something together. "Miss Thomas, I . . ." he looked at her and shook his head. "I have come here today on a specific matter, one of great delicacy."

"Indeed?" She smiled encouragingly at him. Did she have no shame?

He cleared his throat. "Yes. Great delicacy. I do not know how to start. I have a great many things to say to you. I wish to tell you how I . . . feel about you. I mean what I think of you." He rubbed his forehead with the tips of his fingers as though trying to clear his thoughts. When he looked up, she was sitting next to him on the sofa.

She looked directly into his eyes. "I see your struggle to find the words. I can help you. You need not be afraid of saying anything to me." Then she gently put her hand in his.

He stared back at her for a moment, blinking several times. Was she really doing to him what he thought? What he dreaded? He had never been the recipient of such forwardness from a woman before. Never in all his life could he believe that someone who was on the outside all ladylike manners could be so brazen. He had come here today to end a friendship and to try and help his friend – he hadn't expected this.

The exact same thing that had happened to William Risinger.

A wave of revulsion seared though him. He ripped his hand away and stood up to place as much distance between himself and her. The over-furnished room wouldn't allow anywhere near enough.

She looked up at him unsure, and he began to speak. "You're too forward madam. Do you forget your basic manners?"

She shook her head. "Sir, I didn't mean to offend you. I saw your struggles to speak. I wished to help you; to make it easier for you." She spoke in a low tone. So feminine. So soft. The flutter of her eyelids betrayed maiden innocence. Bashfulness. But he knew the truth. It was all a facade.

"Sir, I have . . ." she faltered for a moment, but the desire of her heart pushed her forward and she was no longer afraid to speak. "I have felt for you, from the first moment we met, the strongest attraction, and although it took me some time to realise that I was in love with you, love you I do."

She looked at him to gauge his reaction. He didn't move. But he knew his eyes betrayed the surprise he felt.

"Mr Lucas . . ." she stood up and stepped forward. "Mr Lucas?"

He took a deep breath as if to control a great emotion. "You're mistaken Miss Thomas. You seem to assume that I have come here today to declare my feelings for you," he said with deep frown. "But my feelings couldn't be further from your own."

"I had realised that the strength of your sentiment didn't match my own yet." She stepped forward and placed her hand on his arm. "But I think given time, maybe . . ."

He snatched his arm away from her, and flashed her a piercing look, "Do not touch me."

His angry tone made her frown and then blush. "I'm sorry. I realise that I have said unusual things for a woman. But I have been so long on my own, and without relatives, I find I must do everything for myself."

"You are too forward. You seem to think that I have come here today with a view to –" he struggled to find the words. "A view to intimacy. But I have come here to tell you that you're no longer to see my sister nor any other member of my family."

She stared at him for a few moments and blinked. "I do

not understand. Surely, declaring my sentiments to you couldn't cause you to end my acquaintance with your family?"

"No, my reasons are that I know of your disgusting past and I have come today to tell you how much I dislike you for it."

Louise stood, her mouth gaping open for a moment. "What disgusting past?" Then after a moments' pause she said, "You do not like me?"

"No." There was complete honesty in his voice.

She turned away and remained silent for a few moments. This was not what she was expecting. Disappointment overwhelmed her. It oppressed her. "I do not see how your dislike of me should affect my friendship with Jane. She likes me well enough, even if you do not."

"It's not only my dislike of you that makes me say this. Do you think any moral man of sense would allow his sister to be friends with the likes of you? It's your conduct and the things I have learned about you from William Risinger. I didn't want to believe him, but he was right."

She spun around. "Mr Risinger? What is he to do with it?"

He looked away from her but she caught the look on his face: disgust.

"He has told me the truth about you."

"The truth? Whatever he speaks, I doubt it would be the truth."

"He has told me enough of the matter between the two of you. Your treatment of him. Your unreasonable demands. But you have confirmed everything he told me by your behaviour just now."

She slumped down into the nearest chair. "I cannot see that what happened between Mr Risinger and myself should cause you to demand an end to a friendship. What has he been saying about me?"

"You ask me that?"

"Yes. Tell me what he has said. I demand it."

"I had my doubts for a while, but you confirm everything in your manner and behaviour. He told me about your string of lovers, but I did not think you were capable of it at first."

"Lovers? I have had no lovers. How dare he and you accuse me of such a thing?" Then she muttered, "I should have made him leave immediately."

"You do not deny that you have ordered Mr Risinger out of London?"

"No," she said with a defiant tilt of her chin. "I do not deny it. And if he's not out of London by the deadline I have set, then he will pay dearly."

"I cannot believe I'm hearing this."

"Believe it: for he deserves everything I inflict on him now. He is an evil, conniving man, and the sooner he is gone the better."

Mr Lucas shook his head. "Everything you say makes me dislike you even more." With a hard gaze he continued, "I suppose you will not deny the truth about the child you have kept near your estate?"

Louise went white. "He told you about the child?" she whispered.

"Yes, how you had the child adopted, how you abandoned your own bastard daughter."

Louise shook her head. "I cannot believe he told you about the child, but how did he know? I do not deny that there is a child being brought up in Devon, that I had her adopted out, but Marie is not mine." She gave a small laugh after she stopped speaking as if to add weight to her argument.

He seemed to not hear her last few words. "Yet you have the impertinence to declare yourself to me. To throw yourself at me in the same way you did to Mr Risinger! I thought I had seen and heard it all living in London, but you – you're the worst specimen of a woman I have ever come across."

"I wasn't throwing myself on you." Tears pricked her eyes and she struggled to suppress them.

"You were, and you did. I find it deplorable that you could do such a thing."

"I have no father or brother to assist me in telling you of my favour towards you. I have to do such things myself. But what is wrong with telling you that I love you and that I wish to become your wife?"

He paused and stared at her for a moment. "Then you will be sorry to know that you're furthest in my mind for what constitutes a wife, indeed even a lady."

Her disappointment turned to anger, "Why – because you believe me to be a harlot?"

"Yes."

"You believe Mr Risinger?"

"Yes."

She scoffed, "That man! I should have known the moment I heard he was in your acquaintance that he would cause trouble. He always does. Perhaps you are colluding with him?"

"Colluding to do what?"

"He has never done anything honest in his life. Nothing. Yet I believed you were different. You are at the forefront of your profession, and therefore the world. Why would you seek to become associated with a man with his criminal intent?"

"Criminal? He is no criminal."

"He tried to defraud me a few years ago."

"I do not believe you. I knew him at school and he was a model student. You are simply trying to hide the fact he has uncovered your dark secret."

"No, I am not. How dare he tarnish my character! It is obviously the only way he can get at me now. He is the one who is the liar and I'm sorry to say he has deluded you. Just like he did me."

"I know enough to know when I see a woman who is so rich she believes she can control everything and everyone. You thought you could do the same with me. You're wrong. From the moment I met you, you showed yourself to be a woman who distinguishes herself by embracing those things that make her more male than female. What interest would I have in your estate? Do you think I would have the time, or any inclination to have any desire for it? Do you think I would give up my life's work to become as interfering as you are with your tenants' petty affairs? It would be a half life, a – "

"Stop!" she cried. "Please stop!" Tears now fell freely as she looked up at him. "If you have any compassion for me as a – as a human being, then please I beg you to stop."

He had by no means finished, but for a moment he saw the pathetic creature in front of him, the one Risinger had described, and he halted.

He turned away from her. He knew he had spoken harshly. He had never spoken to a woman in such a way. Perhaps it was his bitter disappointment that she wasn't the woman he once thought she was. It all could have been so different. He had felt an unusual tug of attraction to her all those months ago – even a few minutes ago when he had first entered the room.

He turned back to her. Still her hands were covering her face. He must get this over with quickly. "Miss Thomas, you're not to come to my house or have any contact with any member of my family. Is that clear?"

She nodded.

"Then I shall go. I have done what I meant to do today."

She looked up at him. "And I cannot see how we can continue without further argument. You choose not to believe me and there appears no way I can persuade you otherwise."

11

———

Charles closed the drawing room door and with quick steps made his way to the hallway. The doorman handed him his hat and coat just as the doorbell rang.

"Excuse me sir," the man said and he walked to the door to answer it.

The caller, a blond gentleman, looked familiar, but Charles wasn't inclined to find out who this man might be and, with a quick nod, swiftly left.

"Afternoon Allan," Lord Philip said.

"Adam, sir."

"Is she in? Upstairs?" Without waiting for an answer he made his way up two steps at a time.

The drawing room, where such drama had taken place a few moments ago, was silent except for a quiet sob or two. Lord Philip opened the door, saw his cousin thus occupied and was about to make a hasty retreat, when she looked up and saw him.

"Philip?"

"Er . . ." he tentatively stepped in.

"Philip!" Louise ran into his arms and sobbed a little.

"Whatever is wrong?" He gave her back a tentative pat. "I hope Mr Lucas didn't act ungentlemanly towards you? If he has, I will gladly see him myself and sort things out."

She spoke into his shoulder. "No! No, he has not offended me in that way. We have argued over something, that is all."

"Then he is a brave man to argue with you!"

He took hold of her shoulders and she gave a small smile in response.

"Now what were you arguing about? What could you quarrel about with one of the country's most famous engineers, eh?" Then a thought struck him. "This was nothing to do with Robert Adams, was it?"

"No. Nothing to do with him. I would rather not talk about it."

He led her to the sofa and made her sit.

"Very well, I will not pry. But I'm sure whatever it was, he will come running back to you. What grown man could resist you?"

"You have it wrong . . ."

"Do I?"

Louise shrugged, too tired to argue.

"Philip, you once offered me the convenience of your Paris apartment whenever I chose. Would you mind if I took you up on that offer?"

"What? No, of course I don't mind. You're more than welcome to have it. Paris could be the perfect thing to get over your "argument" with Mr Lucas. Although I'm not sure the City of Love is the ideal place to go?"

Not long after, Louise found herself instructing servants

to pack for France. She wanted to leave as soon as possible, but the inevitable delays of business meant that correspondence had to be undertaken. She wrote to Lucy Potts to ask her to accompany her. If Lucy was willing, and she had little doubt she would be, she decided to travel directly to Dover and meet her there. She wasn't sure she could put up with Lucy for three whole months, but she was willing to try so that she wasn't alone. Besides, her aunt had recently written that Lucy had been receiving attention from a man her parents deemed most unsuitable. It would help to take her away from that and Louise had never felt she had fully discharged her promise to Miss Potts to help Lucy improve and refine herself. If she needed to be alone, Louise would find a way of getting the girl out of her way for a few days or so.

All the arrangements were to be hurried through for her, and a servant sent to collect her and see her to Dover.

Hours later and all that had happened preyed on her mind. Mr Lucas hadn't given her the opportunity to give her side of the story regarding Risinger. She was sure once he knew everything – the truth – that he would at least see his error in believing him. But how to tell him? She could visit him, but it was doubtful she would be able to control her emotions long enough to explain everything. She couldn't bear to see the anger on his face again, or the look in his eyes. It was humiliating enough to think over their argument, she had been caught so unaware by his dislike that she knew it would take a great deal of time to recover. How could she have been so wrong about his feelings for her? It was only at night when fully alone that she saw once again his countenance and heard his words repeated over and over in her mind. Tears fell on more than one occasion, and not only because of the argument, but at the thought that the only man she had ever loved despised her. Why could he not have been the eighth proposal she had received? Why did he so easily believe Mr Risinger? But that man. She herself had been deceived by him too, and it rendered Mr Lucas not so unworthy. If only she had been composed enough to be able to explain everything.

She hoped that once he knew the truth – with evidence – that he would at least believe her and think a little better of her, but she knew that even if that happened he didn't think her suitable as a marriage partner. Her father was wrong: she couldn't marry any single man she chose.

She could write a letter explaining everything. She would take more care over it and explain fully and in every detail. She went to her escritoire and pulled out some paper and started to write a few lines, but the words wouldn't flow. She sat back and rubbed her head. She would have to ensure he would read the letter, if she could finish it. If he knew it was from her, he might toss it into the fire unopened. She would have to take him the letter and make him promise to read it. But that would mean she would have to see his disapproval again. Oh, it was all too vexing.

She could send Lord Philip to explain. He would speak for her, she was certain he would. He could explain everything on her behalf and in an unemotional way. Or she could do a combination and have Lord Philip take the letter and make him read it.

Many hours were spent with these thoughts whirling in her mind. She didn't sleep much, though she was exhausted. In the end, she resolved on a different course of action, and one she decided would be the best.

. . .

Charles went straight home after his interview with Louise. Now that she had been spoken to, it only remained for him to speak to Jane.

His arrival home at such an early hour was an unexpected delight to the female members of the family, although it took a minute for him to persuade them that he wasn't in ill health.

"Mother, would you leave the room? I must speak to Jane in private."

"I cannot see what you have to speak to her about without me knowing. We have no secrets."

"No, but you will find out soon enough. It concerns Miss Thomas."

A thought flooded Mrs Lucas's mind, of course, an engagement had already been formed and he wished to break the news to Jane first because she was her dear friend.

"Very well," she said, and ushered herself out of the room, giving a sly look at Jane as she did.

Jane looked concerned. "Charles, is Louise ill?" she asked.

"No, she is quite well I believe," he stated. "I have been to speak with her." He stood by the fireplace, one hand in his waistcoat pocket.

"What about?"

"Yesterday I learned some extremely grave things about her from Mr Risinger and I have told her that she is to break her friendship with you and not to see you again. She agreed to it, and now I'm telling you: you're not to see her again."

Jane sat motionless, then gave a small laugh. "You're in jest, surely."

"No."

"What did Mr Risinger say?"

He explained their conversation in full and then his most recent discussion with Miss Thomas. "When I mentioned the child, she denied it of course. But she was shocked that I had found out. Jane, I wouldn't ask you to do this without great reason."

"I do not believe you and I do not believe Mr Risinger. A child! I simply do not reckon it, and I shall see my friend as much as I please. I shall speak to her without you telling me whether I can or not. How dare you tell me I can't see her? I will do as I wish."

Charles stood incredulous.

"You will not see her again, Jane. She has a tarnished reputation and I will not stand by and see yours ruined through association with her."

"Her reputation? I have never heard anything of the sort about her. In fact all I ever hear about her is kindness, gentility and purity. Yes, purity. You should not scoff. She is a little eccentric, and her only fault seems to me to be that she is lonely and in need of honest friends who like her for herself and not her wealth. It seems to be only Mr Risinger who has this information. I really do believe he is untruthful. I thought there was something odd about him when I met him. I don't like him, and I can't see how you do."

"Your judgment is clouded by your opinion of Miss Thomas."

"So is yours!"

Neither seemed to be able to back down and they stood and stared at each other for some moments. "Look Jane, I'm not doing this because I want to, but since father died you have been my responsibility and I take it with the utmost seriousness. I realise that I'm not here all the time to watch over you, that work takes me away a great deal, and I'm sorry for it. But I'm adamant on this Jane. You will not see Miss Thomas again."

"And I'm adamant that I shall!"

"Jane . . ." but before he could say anything else she fled the room and left her brother in exasperated solitude.

Jane slammed the front door as she left. In full defiance of her brother, she walked quickly to Louise's house. She arrived and was shown into the hallway straight away.

"I'm afraid Miss Thomas is out," the servant told her in a bland tone.

Jane rather suspected that this wasn't the truth, but she wasn't about to search the rooms herself.

She sighed. "Very well. Will you pass on a message to her?"

"Certainly."

"Tell her that I'm sorry for whatever my stupid brother has said to her and that he is not going to stop me seeing her."

"Yes miss."

"And tell her I'll call back tomorrow morning."

"Miss Thomas is leaving tomorrow for France."

"France?"

"Yes miss."

"Well, tell her that I wish to see her before she leaves."

When Jane arrived home, Charles had gone back to his offices. She recounted the whole sorry argument to her sympathetic mother, who agreed that Louise was beyond doubt a most worthy, virtuous friend and both Charles and Mr Risinger were greatly in error and had used her ill. They then spent hours speculating on why Mr Risinger would make up such stories.

Mrs Lucas was particularly upset at the news of the argument between her son and Miss Thomas. Indeed it was a great let down. She had great plans for the match, although unspoken of to either of her offspring, and she despaired that Charles would ever meet another so worthy, so wealthy and so well-connected. She admitted to herself, however, that Louise's wealth was merely an additional inducement alongside the excellent personal qualities she exhibited. She hoped that all this would quickly blow over and that in time everyone would be friends again.

Two days later and Charles was about to leave for work, when his mother came rushing into the study.

"There is a lawyer here to see you. His name is Mr Russell." Mrs Lucas handed him the card and Charles examined it.

"Did he state his business?"

"No – he just said that he wished to speak to you privately."

Charles sighed. He had planned to get to work early; he had much to do.

"Very well, show him in."

Mrs Lucas disappeared and a few moments later she showed the man in.

Mr Russell was well past middle age, his shoulders stooped. Charles rather wondered why he hadn't retired to the country to enjoy his dotage. He held a large brown leather satchel in one hand, and shook Charles's hand with the other.

"Forgive me this early call, Mr Lucas, but I have come on behalf of my client – Miss Louise Thomas."

"Miss Thomas?" Charles frowned. What would she of all people be doing sending her lawyer? Then he remembered all that William Risinger had told him. She was probably warning him or threatening him in some way.

He sat down and bid Mr Russell to do the same. When

he heard what she wanted, he wanted to be seated. He was ready for a fight.

Mr Russell placed his satchel on the desk and pulled out a large pile of papers. He then delved into his inside jacket pocket and carefully put on his thin silver-coloured spectacles.

"Yes, Miss Thomas wrote to me and asked me to visit you at my earliest convenience. Of course, what with her being one of my prestigious clients, I came immediately."

"Of course," Charles muttered.

Mr Russell sorted the papers onto the desk into separate piles, then looked up at Charles.

"Firstly, she asked me to give you this letter, and make sure you read it."

It was sealed with wax. Charles opened it.

Mr Lucas,

I beg your pardon first for insisting that you read this letter and secondly for anything that I did to offend you the other day. You are the very last person I would wish to displease. I will not, however, apologise for the feelings I expressed yesterday, nor shall I ever mention them again should we ever accidentally meet. You need not fear on that score, I shall do as you wish and stay away from your family.

I have asked my lawyer, Mr Russell, to speak to you on my behalf regarding Mr Risinger. When we spoke, it seemed he had told you a great number of lies. I wish for you to know the truth. With the evidence before you, I hope you will see him for the man he really is.

Louise Thomas

Charles's eyebrows rose. He hadn't expected this. He had thought she would do the same to him as she had done to Risinger – threaten and intimidate him. He looked up at Mr Russell. "Did Miss Thomas tell you what was in the letter?"

"No. She simply asked me to explain a few things to you. She didn't tell me why I was to explain them." He gave a small laugh. "Of course, it's none of my business why she wants me to do this. I'm paid to carry out her wishes, not to gossip."

"Then please go ahead."

12

—————

Mr Russell took off his spectacles and took a deep breath. "Very well. I'll start at the beginning. I believe you went to school with Mr William Risinger and you know him quite well?"

"Yes."

"How much do you know of his late father?"

"Nothing much."

"Then I'll explain. Mr Frederick Risinger was a close friend to Miss Thomas's father. Frederick was a frequent visitor to Glazebrook throughout his life and he and Sir Robert remained friends all their days. Frederick was in the Merchant Navy, and although an officer, never rose above the very basic rank. He was away at sea for much of the time and whilst away asked Sir Robert to watch over his son.

"Sir Robert did this whenever he could, and such was their friendship that Sir Robert paid the boy's school fees, firstly at a school in Plymouth. This place he attended before he went to the same school as you."

"A generous man then," Charles, said thinking back.

This wasn't the picture Risinger had painted of Miss Thomas's father.

"Indeed. However, his duty to watch over William Risinger reached further. Sir Robert was called to the school several times to attend to William, his father being away at sea. Then later, Frederick died. The final time Sir Thomas went there, Willian Risinger was expelled."

"Expelled?"

"Yes. He had been the ringleader of group extorting money from other students. There were other misdemeanours: theft and damage of school property. However, things came to a head when one poor child almost died through punishment for non-payment. William Risinger was given an ultimatum: if he got into trouble again at his new school – the same establishment you attended – he would be sent to the workhouse."

"Are you sure this is what happened?"

"Yes, of course. I have Sir Robert's journal as testament – it's all in there. Besides, I remember it myself. I have, after all, been the Thomas family lawyer nearly all my working life." Mr Russell handed Charles a thick leather journal. "The pages relevant to Mr Risinger have been marked out, as you can see."

Charles looked it over. "I wonder why Miss Thomas keeps the journal with you, and not at home?" he commented. He didn't expect an answer, but Mr Russell was eager to speak.

"She has had the contents copied by scribes. That is the original. I believe she reads it when she feels the need to be closer to her father."

Charles turned to the first marked page. His eyes ran over the details. It was dated 1834. He and Risinger would have been thirteen.

Risinger's criminal past had never been known to him until now. From the journal entry, he was lucky not to have been at the first school. He remembered William arriving at school, but he had told everyone he had changed to be nearer relatives.

He snapped the journal shut. "Forgive me, but crimes committed by a child mean nothing unless the adult has also fallen into such behaviour."

Mr Russell gave a curt nod. "Indeed. In fact, despite these grave mistakes, William remained obedient to the masters at his new school. His somewhat criminal activities put behind him, he appeared to have turned over a new leaf. Sir Robert was glad of it.

"Nothing happened with William Risinger for the rest of his days at school, and now I must move to the time when Sir Robert died."

"Go ahead." From what Risinger had told him, this would be the interesting part.

"Miss Thomas knew of her father's wish to help Mr Risinger and decided to continue to provide for his education. By this time he was a full year into his studies at Oxford. She visited him there to tell him of this, and the two soon became friends.

"After Mr Risinger left Oxford and started in trade, their friendship deepened and they were like brother and sister. He helped her with her business matters and advised her whenever she asked. She trusted him. You may have noticed that Miss Thomas is somewhat solitary? Some might even call her ... lonely."

Charles remembered that Jane had used the same words. "Yes, I suppose she could be described that way."

"She was delighted to have Mr Risinger as a trusted friend and when he turned 25, she decided as a last gesture to the memory of her father to help him in one final way. She had me draw up a contract stipulating that should he ever marry, he would receive in Sir Robert's name the sum of five thousand pounds. Another generous gesture, wouldn't you agree?"

"Undoubtedly," Charles said in a low murmur. He couldn't say much else. This was very different to the story Risinger had told him.

"Now is the interesting part of the story. Miss Thomas told him of the gift and she saw little of him for six months."

"Why stay away so long?"

"Exactly! He told Miss Thomas business kept him away, but the blackguard was up to no good. One night, about eight months after her promise of the money, she was visited by a young woman who used to be in her service. She had married the landlord of an inn many miles away from Glazebrook. This woman told Miss Thomas that on the previous night, Mr Risinger had been in her inn talking furtively with a few other men about how he had advised her to invest in many under-hand schemes and that he was leading up to getting me to invest a considerable sum of money. He wanted to take as much money from her as possible, in order to lead to her downfall and even force her to sell her ancestral home."

Charles sat motionless. Surely this was not true?

Mr Russell continued. "Miss Thomas's reaction was, of course, to doubt this woman, but she decided to investigate all the same. How could she not?"

"Indeed." Charles's mind was almost unable to compre-hend what he had just heard. If this was what had really happened, he had made a grave mistake. But then, Miss Thomas had said Risinger had tried to defraud her.

"She came to me, and I employed a private investigator.

Nearly a month later, I obtained material proof that Mr Risinger was in fact leading her into bad investments. He borrowed money from several people to pay her, to show that his advice in investments yielded profit."

Charles swallowed, his throat was dry. "What happened next?"

"She confronted Mr Risinger of course, and he denied everything at first, but after she showed him the evidence his reaction was extreme. It took four of her strongest servants to restrain him; but not after he had struck her several times."

"He did that?"

Mr Russell leaned forward and took a pen between his long thin fingers. "I saw her the day after he was taken into custody, and she had terrible bruises on her face where he hit her. He was completely unrepentant. She was far too lenient with him, in my opinion. Should have had him locked up. The fraud alone would have given him at least fifteen years in prison, possibly transportation, and the evidence was overwhelming. Still, it was her decision. I'm sure a man wouldn't have been so charitable."

"Why would he do that to her?" Charles whispered.

"He wanted her estate, her money. He even stated it openly; he said as Sir Robert's only godson, he should have the right to her inheritance."

"A strange idea."

"Yes, but even stranger given that Sir Robert wasn't Mr Risinger's godfather, though he had been as generous as one."

Mr Russell sat back in his chair. "His intention all along had been to get Miss Thomas to marry him so that he could obtain her estate. He realised that the gift of five thousand pounds was the final proof that she didn't consider marriage with him."

"Perhaps he didn't believe her," Charles said, suddenly realising he believed her now and not his friend. "Or denied to himself that she felt anything other than platonic sentiments towards him. Maybe he believed that over time she would fall in love with him."

"Perhaps," Mr Russell acknowledged.

"What happened next?" Charles found himself asking.

"After the servants restrained him, the local magistrate was called, and he was taken into custody. After much discussion, he agreed to leave the country for good, if Miss Thomas wouldn't press charges. He wanted to go to France. What to do, I know not, but he was to leave immediately. He was escorted to Calais, and then on to a train headed for Paris, and he was gone.

"Miss Thomas saw nothing of Mr Risinger until that day in your house. We believed him still in France, true to the agreement."

"She told you they met here?"

"Yes, she summoned me that day. She also asked me to show you the affidavit Risinger signed admitting his guilt."

It took some minutes for Charles to read the paper; the words swirled. "His crimes are grievous," he said eventually.

"Yes, but they do not stop there."

Charles looked up. "There is more?"

Mr Russell nodded. "Miss Thomas has asked me to explain about the child. She believed Mr Risinger had made you believe it was hers?" Mr Russell gave a small laugh.

"That is what he told me, yes." Charles went cold. He was sure he was about to be told the child was not hers.

"Soon after he was released from custody and in France, Mr Risinger, anxious that Miss Thomas might cancel the contract on his marriage, sought out a dying widow who agreed to marry him.

"This woman, who was with child by her recently deceased husband, married Mr Risinger so he could obtain the money, and in return, he promised to look after the child as his own. The marriage took place, and soon after the child was born, the mother passed away. However, Mr Risinger, having received his money, left the woman many weeks before and did nothing to look after the child. He has, I believe, never seen the child, and although he is the legal father, named as such quite legally on the birth certificate, he has never honoured his promise to his wife.

"Miss Thomas visited the grandparents, who confirmed the abandonment. They themselves, being infirm, were not capable of looking after the child, so Miss Thomas graciously asked if she could place the child with a loving but childless couple near Glazebrook, who agreed to look after her as their own. The child has now been legally adopted by them and is very happy. Mr Risinger can never have any claim on her; something that Miss Thomas was eager to ensure, given his previous behaviour."

Mr Russell handed Charles several papers: a birth certificate of a child, "Marie Annette Risinger", and adoption papers, several of which were in French.

"It's a mystery how Mr Risinger found out that the baby was adopted out." Mr Russell stared at Charles. "Though, given the amount of gossip that goes about London, it's no small wonder."

Charles took a deep breath. He had never heard any gossip, but then, he wasn't the sort of man who was interested in it. It was only Risinger who had ever told him of Miss Thomas.

Mr Russell continued again. "I must warn you in the

strongest possible terms against any further involvement with Mr Risinger, either personally or in business. He has proved himself to be dishonourable, dishonest and completely untrustworthy."

Charles pulled at his shirt collar. He suddenly felt ashamed. She was in the right. Absolved of everything. Innocent. Sudden regret swamped him. He had acted unreasonably towards her, accused her and believed Risinger. He had been hasty, irrational and stupid.

Mr Russell spoke again. "I have to say Mr Lucas, I was surprised when Miss Thomas gave me leave to let you see these papers, though not in the way you may think. In fact, I was rather pleased that she has told someone else about Mr Risinger. She keeps things so close and has only ever told one other person, her cousin Lord Philip Eldon, and he's not much help. She shuts herself away from society so much these days. She does have dinners and attends parties but there is no one she is really close to. There was a time she wouldn't come near London because she was pursued by fortune hunters. But it's nice to know she's made friends with such an eminent person as yourself. In fact, it's an honour to meet you."

He paused briefly before he continued. "I have known her a long time you see, since she was a girl, and she was always an excellent child. She has many responsibilities and sometimes they appear to weigh her down considerably, but I'm sure you know that. It's not an easy task running an estate as large as hers these days, especially with so much change going on in the world. Yes, I'm glad that you know these details, it will at least be good for her to have another confidant in this matter. She hasn't told you about Mr Robert Adams, then?"

Mr Russell's sudden change of subject surprised him. "Mr Adams? No." Charles shook his head.

"No, I didn't think so. I just thought she might have done, what with Mr Adams investing so much in your work. But I've said too much already." He held up his hands.

This last comment silenced Mr Russell henceforth and he said nothing more for some time as Charles gave the papers one more glance, to imprint everything on his mind.

Mr Russell's earlier speech about Miss Thomas didn't help the overwhelming feeling of guilt Charles now had. He was utterly and completely wrong. Now he didn't know what to do. His mind moved to the other accusations he laid at her door, including his charge of unladylike behaviour. He still considered what she had done as highly unusual, even though she had been exonerated of Risinger's lies. But lies they were and he felt somewhat embarrassed at having believed them.

The knowledge that he had aroused such a physical response in her was still a little strange. He had never been a romantic man, and couldn't understand these feelings that she professed to have. Had his earlier feelings for her been love?

His thoughts were intruded on by Mr Russell's monotonous voice. "I don't suppose you have heard the latest goings on with Mr Risinger?"

"That he is to go to America?"

"Yes, but more than that. We had word this morning that he has disappeared."

"Disappeared?" Concern spread across Charles's face.

"Yes. He was being watched of course; Miss Thomas saw to that a while ago. No, what I mean is he gave the men who watched him the slip the other night. Not sure how he managed it, but he's definitely gone, the blighter."

"Does Miss Thomas know?"

Mr Russell delved into his waistcoat pocket and pulled out a silver watch. "Yes, by now the man sent to tell her will have reached her. She's on her way to France. But I'm sure you know that."

Charles nodded. Jane had told him.

"And what is being done to find him?" Charles felt a sudden agitation and he wasn't sure why.

"We have many men looking for him. Don't concern yourself too much. No expense will be spared to find him."

"And what about Miss Thomas's safety? He attacked her once before. Should there not be extra men to protect her? And the child too? Should she not be taken somewhere safe until he is found?"

Mr Russell sat back in his chair. "Yes. You're right. Thank you for your concern. A true friend to Miss Thomas! I think that is an excellent idea. I shall arrange it immediately. Extra protection is exactly what she needs."

After a short pause, Charles spoke again. "If there is anything I can do to assist you, please let me know, even the smallest thing."

"Thank you Mr Lucas, although I wouldn't want to trouble such a busy man as yourself."

"It's no trouble. I insist. If there is anything I can do, please tell me."

"Of course." Mr Russell smiled and his cool gaze settled on Charles for a moment.

Mr Russell left soon after, and Charles's thoughts were in turmoil. Part of him shrank away from the grave mistake he had made: it was mortifying. He had been so rude to Miss Thomas, both at her own house and his. The other part, the stronger part of him, knew that he must beg Miss Thomas's pardon for what he had done. He had to do it, as a gentleman. This would be a little more difficult with her on her way to France, so being the practical man he was, he knew what he must do.

He called at Miss Thomas's house to enquire after an address to write to her. He was told by her assistant that his mistress had expressly asked him to open all letters and return any of them that were from the Lucas family. The man was adamant that he was to follow her instructions, for to disobey his kind and thoughtful employer wasn't to be contemplated. Charles even tried to bribe the man, but received a cutting response. The man was too loyal to even do that, saying that no amount of money would make him betray his mistress. It seemed the man was to receive a generous pension from her, and he wasn't willing to jeopardise it.

Charles asked if he could be informed of her return, but the assistant didn't know, or at least that is what he said. He suspected that he didn't wish to tell him. In any case, the man was leaving that day to join his employer in France, and therefore trying to get a letter to Miss Thomas through the lawyer would prove a fruitless endeavour. The assistant would be in France before it.

He left her house agitated, and annoyed that any letter would be returned, because it was his own fault. He had desired all contact with his family to be at an end, and she was simply following his wishes.

That evening, when their mother had retired, Charles told Jane of the things he had learned about Louise. Jane sat silent and grave as she listened to him, until he told her of the child, and then she was no longer able to keep quiet.

"Did I not tell you Miss Thomas was of an exemplary character? What a mess you have created for me. Look how foolish you have been!"

"Yes, foolish is probably the correct word for it," he said in a serious tone.

"I have always been a much better judge of character than you," Jane said. "I thought there was something sinister about Mr Risinger. I'm very angry at you, Charles. My dear friend has been treated badly. Think how upset she must be."

Charles didn't dare mention the fact that Miss Thomas had declared her wish to marry him. What Jane would say to that, he could guess. She would most likely tell him that he was a fool to turn her down and that he didn't deserve the attentions of a woman so much better than he. She was probably right.

Jane continued on. "I feel the loss of my friend greatly. Despite the infrequency of our time spent together, I have grown fond of Louise. I'm still angry with you, but what is done is done, and now I have to look forward and help you gain pardon for any wrongdoing. I'm sure in time I will forgive you completely. I suppose you can't help your lack of intuition regarding the character of men and women. The problem is your engineering-like approach to life. You would get along better in life if men and women were machines."

Ordinarily, Charles would have defended himself, but not today. "I'm trying to correct the situation. I have tried and will continue to try to speak to Miss Thomas to ask her forgiveness."

"Good. Not that you deserve it."

"I know. But I have to try."

Jane touched his arm in an affectionate gesture. "If I know Louise, she will forgive you."

Charles's spirits lifted. "You think she will?"

"Yes."

The next day, Mrs Lucas was included in the information her son had brought. Jane told her everything, but Mrs Lucas wouldn't be drawn into expressing an opinion of censure for her son. An opinionated woman, she still had designs on a match between her son and Miss Thomas, and kept to her hope that this might still happen.

13

The messenger who carried the letter telling Louise of Mr Risinger's disappearance reached her just after she arrived at Dover. She was shocked, dismayed and angry at the news, but part of her wasn't completely surprised that something had happened. She rued the day she had ever contacted Mr Risinger after her father died. If she had ever thought all this would happen especially now, to top everything else.

She was glad Mr Russell had made all necessary arrangements to find Risinger again and she found there was little for her to do, except worry. It would be at least a day until Lucy arrived at Dover and they could make the crossing, so her thoughts preyed on her. She couldn't understand why Mr Risinger could possibly want to disappear. She had paid for his passage to America and it was he who wanted to go there. Previously, in such troubled times, in order to help her mental state, she would have dwelt upon Mr Lucas as a respite. But not now. She wasn't sure which of the two men made her more unhappy. Instead she busied herself with small outings around Dover to make the time move faster.

The next day she received another letter from Mr Russell that stated that he believed it a good idea for her to have more protection around her, and that his investigations now showed that Mr Risinger had disappeared because of pressing debts; so pressing that he couldn't wait for his passage to America. He feared that the port was being watched and he would be prevented from leaving. It intrigued her how he could have spent the five thousand pounds that he had received from her in such a short period of time, but she was even more annoyed that Mr Russell's advice was for her to pay off the man's debts so that he could surface. She wasn't willing to do it. The debts, according to Mr Russell, amounted to at least a thousand pounds and there were possibly more. No, at this stage she wouldn't and she was sure that Mr Risinger could be found without any unnecessary expense. Besides, if she did this now, what was to stop him doing the same thing again and in America? She wouldn't pay the price for his mistakes again.

Lucy arrived in Dover the day after Louise, and in a most excited state. Ordinarily, Louise would have found her exasperating. But this time an over-eager traveling companion, overwhelmed with gratitude, was what she needed to take her mind off recent events. It was simple – she needed someone who looked up to her and made her feel wanted again.

They sailed for Calais the next day and were to stay in Paris for three months. Louise looked forward to improving her French, which hadn't been used much lately. Lucy was also proficient in the language, so the two of them were well-prepared.

Lord Philip's apartment was situated in a respectable suburb of Paris and gave the two ladies an excellent base to explore not only the city itself, but the surrounding area. They had no acquaintances in Paris, but Lord Philip had asked several of his friends to call upon them, and soon they were frequently invited to balls, card parties and dinners.

Louise never forgot the reason she was there. She had erred in forwarding herself to Mr Lucas. She had been stupid to speak of her feelings in such a way – no lady of sense would have done it. But she excused herself because of her feelings. Her love for him had made rational behaviour impossible and she was so used to getting what she desired – and she desired and loved him more than anyone else. She had to get on with her life and try to forget him, however difficult it might be.

She learned to hide all contemplations of Mr Lucas. She didn't ask Mr Russell of his visit to Mr Lucas in her letter. She just hoped that having learned the truth, he would at least think a little better of her and acquit her of his objections. No gentleman she met in Paris could match him. He was the standard to which she compared every man. None were as handsome, none as clever, none drew her attention in a room in the same way he had done. It was something that she couldn't stop herself from doing. It had become part of her.

Her mortification over all that passed between them was still apparent. She couldn't believe how wrong she had been about his feelings. She felt very naive, childlike even. She wasn't sure that she would ever get over the look of disgust on his face. It tortured her. She had never been told she was unladylike by anyone. She examined her own behaviour in every situation and asked herself if she was indeed doing anything wrong. She knew his comment must be based on something Mr Risinger had said, that he believed her to be free with her affections. But still there was the long list of other objections: that he thought her more male than female, that she was furthest in his mind from what constituted a wife. What did he want in a wife? Could she ever match it?

When the three months in Paris was over, Louise and Lucy both found themselves wondering where the time had gone, and they reluctantly made their way back to England. Standing at the docks in Calais, Louise watched Lucy as their ship prepared itself for the voyage. Lucy was dressed in a beautiful blue muslin gown, one of the best Paris had to offer. She had grown in maturity since the day they had left, though she could never be a friend in the same way Jane had been. With Jane there was an easiness of dialogue and they seemed to understand each other without speaking. Despite being only a few years younger than Jane, Lucy needed many things explained. She had grown up in a sheltered, protected way. When asked about her parents, she merely spoke of them in terms of their age, appearance and position in life and barely mentioned them otherwise.

Louise had at times found Lucy somewhat difficult to be with – her flighty nature could be exasperating. But then her mind would wander back to the reason why they were in Paris and she would check herself.

Luckily, Lucy spoke of Mr Francis only twice. Both times she managed not to cry and only to say that she hoped he was well and had found a position. If her mind dwelt on him at other times, she gave no indication.

They parted in London. Lucy had hoped that her illustrious friend would invite her to stay in London for a few weeks, but it wasn't to be.

Louise arrived back at her estate somewhat at ease, but

her three months away meant a backlog of work. Although her steward took care of many issues, there was always a list of things that only she could decide. She threw herself into those tasks as earnestly as ever.

There was still no news of Mr Risinger. Mr Russell pressed her to pay off the man's debts. The child was hidden in a safe place, and she still felt a reluctance to do anything regarding this man. If Mr Risinger hadn't purposely turned Mr Lucas against her, perhaps she would have acted more kindly towards him. But she hated him more for his recent actions than ever before.

. . .

In those same months while Louise was in Paris, Charles had written to Mr Russell to offer the child Marie sanctuary in Scotland with his aunt. It was declined because arrangements for the child's removal from Devon had already been made, but Mr Russell was affable with thanks in his reply.

Charles was a little frustrated that he hadn't means of assistance in this situation and that he was still unable to make an apology. Any mention of Miss Thomas to Jane would cause her to be quiet for many hours afterwards. He resumed work, but often found himself thinking of the safety of both the child and Miss Thomas. There was much work to do; a commission for a viaduct in West London meant that he had little time for other projects. The Tamar bridge progressed well, but he decided that now was a good time to call Mr Boyd back from Devon. His visit would serve three purposes: to update his employers more fully about the progress of the bridge, for the employers to offer him a partnership, and most importantly, as a distraction for Jane.

When Mr Boyd returned to London, Jane spent many of her evenings in his company. Her brother's diversion may have worked, but she still missed her friend.

On one such evening as they all sat together, Ashton took a gulp of port and placed his glass down. "It seems we have a problem with some of the funding for the Tamar bridge."

"What is it?" Charles asked.

"One of the major investors has dropped out."

"Who?"

"Mr Townend. I've never met him, but it seems his promise of money has never materialised."

"You don't seem concerned."

"I am a little. There were others interested in investing, but we could run into serious problems soon if we don't get the cash quickly. We may even have to stop the work. One of the interested investors who was too late for the funding the first time around was Robert Adams. I contacted him recently about Boyd becoming a partner, but the letter was returned. I sent an update on the progress of his main investment, the Bristol Docks enlargement, but that too was returned. I know he was interested in the bridge, but it seems I have no way of contacting him at the moment."

Charles stopped for a moment. "You might want to speak to a lawyer in Bond Street. He might be able to help. His name is Mr Russell and I believe he might be able to get you in contact with Mr Adams."

"Very well. I will try," Ashton replied.

"Tell me – Mr Adams, he hasn't withdrawn funding from our other projects?" Charles wondered whether Miss Thomas had contacted Mr Adams and asked him to remove his support.

"No. Only that he returns my letters. Do not worry," Ashton said. "These things have a way of sorting themselves out."

Charles gave a slow nod and watched his sister and Boyd

near the fire. What they spoke about he couldn't hear, but for the first time in his life he found their intimacy intriguing. They were seated a respectable distance apart, both blushed frequently and Jane, despite her impeccable self control, looked at Boyd in a way she obviously reserved just for him. Charles was more than happy about the match and he felt a declaration would happen soon. He hoped that it would remove the slight awkwardness that remained between him and his sister. He shifted himself in his chair as he thought yet again of Mr Risinger. He hadn't heard anything from Mr Russell for many weeks and could only assume that he hadn't been found.

One week later, Lucas, Ashton and their new partner Boyd left London for the Tamar bridge in Devon.

"We will need to stop off at Axminster, and we may need to stay there for one night. Mr Russell, that lawyer, was helpful in pointing me in the right direction of Mr Adams," Ashton said as the train made its way out of London.

Hours later they arrived at Axminster, a pleasant little station close to the town centre. Only just over the border from Dorset, it was lush, clean and quiet. They found rooms at the inn closest to the station and then hired a cab. Ashton insisted both partners accompany him to their destination. He was hopeful of meeting Mr Adams and wanted them with him to impress him and explain anything he might ask.

An hour later they found themselves being driven past a grand Portland stone gateway arch and gatehouse.

The road to the grand house they expected to see any moment seemed to go on for miles. Finally, the view changed from forest to meadow and then landscaped gardens. Then, there it stood: the estate house that Ashton hoped would lead him to Mr Adams.

The front door was answered by the porter, who after hearing from Ashton in hushed tones, showed them into a huge room that they all took to be the drawing room. It was furnished with red Indian silk wallpaper, a large Persian carpet and the finest French chairs. There were several portraits on the walls and on the tables stood huge, finely decorated porcelain vases. It was truly the house of someone of considerable wealth.

The servant returned a few minutes later. "Miss Thomas will see you shortly," he said, and then closed the door.

Charles's heart almost stopped. "Miss Thomas?" he said in a strangled voice.

"Yes, thought I would keep it secret from you until the last possible moment. I know she's not your favourite member of the gentry," Ashton said slyly. "Didn't want you refusing to come. She is our last hope of contact with Mr Adams. I always believed she had a preference for you or at least that her interest in engineering made her a little in awe of you."

In all the years Ashton had known him, he had never seen Charles look so shocked. He seemed to want to speak, but couldn't utter a single word. He seemed to want to leave, but couldn't move.

"How could you?" he managed.

Ashton held up his hands. "Now, now Charles, try not to be annoyed – it's all for the partnership, you know. Bear it as well as you can. Hopefully it will be a short visit. She can tell us how to contact Mr Adams and we shall be on our way."

Charles went pale. He grasped a nearby table. Until he remembered it was her table in her house. Fear and dread over came him in waves, as well as the knowledge that had he sought such an interview for three months, but never expected it at such short notice. His mind raced as to what to say.

He wondered how he would be received. By now she would know he was here. He had given his card to the porter along with his partners.

14

One of the footmen told Louise of the three gentlemen's arrival. "I will be down in due course," she said, without a note of emotion. The door clicked shut and she suddenly felt very alone. She had to stop herself from shaking. Finally they were here. Well versed as she was to receiving visitors, she had never received a man she loved here in Devon. Yes, she still loved him despite all that had passed between them and her best efforts to forget him. It would be sweet turmoil, with her knowledge of his dislike for her and for landowners such as she. But part of her wouldn't allow his feelings to remove the fact that she ran her estate as she saw fit and she ran it well. No, he may dislike what she represented, he may dislike her for her behaviour, but she would never be ashamed of her ancestry and the great privilege in life that she had inherited.

Still, there was an awkwardness about her. She told herself she must appear as ladylike as possible; that his objections to her were such that she must demonstrate a high level of propriety. She paced the room for several minutes and muttered to herself, as she tried to gain her composure.

She knew of their arrival, had expected it. She had received Mr Russell's letter a few days ago:

I trust this letter finds you well. I have no news of Risinger, but will inform you of any further developments. We still believe him to be in Manchester or Liverpool and are taking all necessary measures. The child is safe and well.

I write this time on a different matter. Yesterday I was visited by Mr Ashton, of Lucas and Ashton Partnership. He informed me he was trying to contact Robert Adams, but that all recent letters had been returned. I thought it a little odd that this should happen and that you would have informed me of Mr Adams's withdrawal of funding etc to this company. I therefore gave him leave to contact you directly, your previous trust of Mr Lucas being my major motive in allowing this unusual occurrence. That gentleman has certainly taken a keen interest in the disappearance of Mr Risinger and has offered his help to find him.

I haven't told him anything other than the fact that you can give him information on Mr Adams, so if you choose not to take the final step to reveal – you can say you're Mr Adams's agent, or such. Mr Ashton and his partners intend to call on you on their way to the Tamar bridge works in a few days' time.

I hope I haven't been too presumptuous in any of these actions.

Etc

Mr Russell gave little away, but the news that Mr Lucas appeared to believe her side of the story gave her great solace. She checked her image in the mirror. She looked well enough: her hair tied expertly, her dress of light pink cotton, one of the newer ones purchased in Paris. It was very becoming, the height of fashion. Not that he would notice.

That was her only regret. She could be the most beautiful woman in the world and he wouldn't care.

Finally, she found herself opening the drawing room door and stepping in.

The three gentlemen were standing in different places around the room. Mr Ashton was the nearest and, upon seeing her enter, stepped forward to greet her.

"How do you do?" she curtsied.

He took her outstretched hand. "Well. Thank you, Miss Thomas, I am very pleased to see you again. I hope you do not mind our intrusion, but we come on business."

"Not at all," she said.

"You know Mr Lucas of course." She turned to where Mr Ashton indicated and allowed herself to look at him. He looked well; his hair was longer than usual and his complexion was clear and bright. But it was his eyes that showed the truth, they were dark and assessing. To her disappointment he didn't move closer and remained the six or seven steps away. His distance only served as a reminder that she had missed his tall, handsome figure in a room.

"Mr Lucas, I'm very pleased to see you again."

"Miss Thomas," he replied with a bow, and kept his gaze on her.

"How are your mother and sister?"

"They are well, thank you," he replied.

"I . . . I'm glad of it." She paused to try and stop her blushes, before she continued with great composure, "Will you give them my best regards when you see them next?"

"Of course," he said, then looked away. Their conversation was now over, it seemed. She took it to mean that he no longer wished to talk to her and disappointment surged through her. She had hoped things would be different between them despite their last conversation, but it appeared nothing had changed. Had he read her letter? Had he listened to all that Mr Russell had told him? Maybe he still blamed her. Maybe, despite everything, he disliked her so much that nothing could counter it.

Mr Ashton then continued, "And this is Mr Henry Boyd, our new partner."

"I'm pleased to make your acquaintance," she said.

Mr Boyd was a handsome man by any standards and his manner seemed pleasing. He was young, no more than twenty-five, and taller than the others. His frame was large but though in some this would cause clumsiness, Mr Boyd held himself well. Jane had excellent taste. But she expected nothing less. She recollected herself. "I believe you're all here to see Mr Adams?"

"Yes. Is there some way we can get a message to him? We would like to speak to him," Ashton said.

"Mr Adams is not available, but anything you wish to say to him can be said to me. I'm his agent."

Louise saw Ashton steal a sly glance at Mr Lucas, as if unsure what to say next. He drew himself up. "I hope you do not think me rude, but we really would prefer to speak to Mr Adams directly. Would you tell me how I can contact him?" He gave an apologetic smile.

"I'm afraid that is not possible." She tilted up her chin, daring him to question her further.

"We have urgent business," Ashton said. "And in order to protect Mr Adams's investments, we must speak with him. Our letters have been returned and you are our only means of contact with him."

"And I'm telling you that he is not available and you must speak to me." She tried to remain polite, though she was starting to grow annoyed.

Ashton seemed to sense her irritation and cleared his

throat. "Forgive me madam, but how can we be sure that Mr Adams has you as his proxy in these matters?"

She thought for a moment. He had a point. It seemed there was no way around this. She trusted two out of the three, but wasn't entirely sure whether she should run such a risk in disclosing the vital information to the third.

"Mr Boyd is an equal partner now, you said?"

"Yes,"

"All the necessary paperwork for this has been completed and signed?"

"Yes, it was completed more than a month ago. May I enquire as to where these questions are leading?"

"Merely, I needed to ascertain whether Mr Boyd could be trusted to keep Mr Adams's secret. As a partner he will lose too much if he divulges anything."

"What secret might that be?" Ashton asked.

"I am Robert Adams."

Silence descended on the room after her words were spoken. She hoped someone would say something, but no one did. Louise watched as Ashton looked at his partners, obviously hoping they would speak. Both Mr Lucas and Mr Boyd seemed stunned into silence. Eventually, after Ashton shifted about a little, he asked, "You are Robert Adams?"

"Yes," she said. "We're one and the same. Robert Adams is the name I use for my investments. I'm sorry your letters were returned by my assistant; it seems he followed my request too stringently. When I told him to return any letters from Mr Lucas and his family, I didn't mean him to include business letters to Robert Adams. But it's my own fault, I should have been more specific."

They all seemed to ignore her last comment, or at least, not take it in.

Ashton cleared his throat. "Forgive me if I doubt you, but

I find this all a little unusual. You're saying that you and Robert Adams are the same person?"

"Yes."

Charles stepped forwards, his face a little paler than a few moments before, "Ashton – I know enough of Miss Thomas to know she always speaks the truth." Then he added, "However strange it may seem."

Louise met his gaze and said in genuine gratitude, "Thank you."

"Well then, it must be true. But why were you returning Charles's letters?" Ashton asked.

She opened her mouth to speak when Mr Lucas interrupted. "It was a misunderstanding between us, for which I'm most earnestly sorry now. I have been for the last three months, even before your news a moment ago."

She searched his face for truthfulness. She saw what she hoped to see. "Thank you."

"Well Mr Adams, can we adjourn somewhere and speak of business matters?" Ashton asked with a smile.

"Of course, please come with me to the study."

She led them all to a large oak-panelled room and sat behind a vast oak desk that was covered with piles of paper and folders. The blotting paper was covered with ink spots, and at the side was a pile of pens and pencils. Discussions began, and before long it became clear that Lucas and Boyd were not needed. She suggested they walk about the grounds so that she could negotiate alone with Ashton.

"We're only half a mile from the coast," she said, "and there is a pleasant walk that way. On a clear day like today, you can see Portland."

They agreed and departed once one of the servants arrived to show them the way, and the negotiations resumed. She was a little relieved to have Mr Lucas away for a time. His presence was oppressive and she found it difficult to concentrate on business matters, yet strangely as soon as he was gone she wished him returned. What must he think of her now?

Ashton spoke to Miss Thomas in an honest and forthright manner about the bridge and why further investment was needed. She listened intently as he explained the percentage of the toll price she could expect to get for her investment. She was eager to invest, having offered before as Robert Adams, but was too late the first time around. However, as an accomplished businesswoman, she knew not to let her eagerness show. She wanted a higher percentage of the toll charges but would settle for less if she had to. In the end, the agreed details would be advantageous to both.

When the negotiations seemed to have been resolved, she looked out of the window. The sky was dark and a few droplets of rain fell.

"I do hope Mr Lucas and Mr Boyd are not caught out in that rain. Now I feel sorry I sent them outside. I should have directed them to the billiard room instead."

"A bit of rain never hurt anyone!" Ashton got up and stood beside her. "Besides, Mr Lucas is a terrible billiards player and would probably have ripped the cloth on the table."

She couldn't help but smile. So, there was something Mr Lucas was bad at. "I shall call for tea, so that on their return they can at least be refreshed."

The ramblers returned fifteen minutes later, only slightly wet, and were greeted with the happy news that Robert Adams was to invest in the bridge.

"If I were a gentleman, I would offer to shake your hand on it," she said.

"I will shake your hand as a lady, that is enough," and Ashton held out his hand.

She moved her hand as if she was about to offer it back, but suddenly, she looked at Mr Lucas and remembered his words "you're more male than female'. She pulled her hand back. Then she turned around and walked to the window and seemingly looked out, with a deep sigh.

"Miss Thomas?" Ashton asked.

She heard him, but didn't move.

"Miss Thomas is anything wrong?" he persisted. "Have I said something to offend you?" He spoke in a concerned tone.

She forced her mind to stop dwelling on such painful memories, turned around in a hurried manner and said in a serious tone. "I give you my word, and it will have to be good enough".

The confused mood of the room was lightened by the arrival of tea a few minutes later. Mr Ashton was unsure what he had said to offend, Mr Boyd was blissfully unaware of any awkwardness and Mr Lucas felt it keenly that Miss Thomas was avoiding speaking to him. She had barely spoken to him, other than what was necessary, and avoided his gaze.

He knew he deserved no special treatment, yet he felt a little shameful being in her house, drinking her tea and taking her money for investment after everything he had said to her that day. He must try and speak to her to make amends properly.

The walk with Boyd had been pleasant – more than pleasant. They went to the coast as directed and the sea air refreshed him after their long journey. It was a beautiful part of the country. Stunning. Unique. Besides that, he was barely able to comprehend everything he had learned: that she took his verbal abuse as she declared her love, all the time she knew she was the one who played a major part in his work as an investor called Robert Adams.

She was Robert Adams. It had taken him aback the moment she said the words. But though he was surprised, he didn't doubt her. No, not now. He would never doubt her again.

So that was what Mr Russell, her lawyer, had alluded to those months ago when he had visited. She had given him leave to know the situation behind her dealings with William Risinger, but not this other secret. He looked over to her. She was an exceptional woman. He always thought she was, it was only Risinger's lies that had made him think the worst of her – and he was foolish enough to believe him. He scolded himself again. He must make amends.

Over these thoughts, he heard Miss Thomas ask them all to dinner that evening, and Ashton accept on their behalf.

"The food at the inn in Axminster is excellent I believe," she said. "But I would be honoured if you would return later, to save me dining alone tonight if nothing else."

"But it's such late notice. Will not your cook be angry?" Ashton asked.

"My domestic staff are among the best in the county and are prepared for late requests; but you forget, I knew you were coming today."

Charles knew he deserved no special attention from her, but perhaps she might forgive him after all. She certainly seemed gracious enough to be kind to him after his behaviour to her.

Mr Boyd asked, "Miss Thomas, I'm intrigued as to why you use a different name for your investments. Is there a reason for it?"

She placed her teacup down. "I will attempt to explain. It's not the greatest secret ever kept; in fact, several other of the companies and partners I invest in already know I'm Mr Adams. But there are some people – one person – who wishes me ill and he almost did me a great deal of harm. It's for that reason primarily that I took the name."

She continued after a pause. "That is why you must not speak of this to anyone. It could harm your work if this man finds out." She looked directly at Mr Lucas. He knew whom she was speaking of: William Risinger. She hid her investments because of him. How much harm had he done her that she had resorted to hiding her identity?

Her tone became lighter. "But despite this, I found after a while that it's refreshing being known as a man, especially when I receive business correspondence. I'm afraid that before Robert Adams I found businessmen condescending when they wrote to me. They thought me stupid I'm sure, and in need of a large amount of explanation for anything remotely technical. I trust your reports will not change in tone now you know? I would be very disappointed if they did."

Ashton shook his head. "Of course not. But it gives new meaning to the questions you received at your dinner last year when you were asked whether Mr Adams was to attend."

"Yes, although Mr Stephenson is fully aware that I am Robert Adams. It amuses him to mention him whenever he can."

"What made you choose the name 'Robert Adams'?" Charles asked.

She turned to him at last. "Robert was my father's name. Adams was my mother's maiden name. There are portraits of them over there." She pointed to the corner of the room and they all looked over. Amongst a number of landscape paintings was a portrait of a man and woman. The woman was seated and the man stood beside her. Charles hadn't noticed them before among the finery of the room. Her parents' portrait was a fine piece of art. She looked like her mother – except more beautiful.

"A sensible choice," Ashton commented as Boyd walked over to the pictures. "I see no portrait of you?"

She went over to Boyd and stood gazing up at the picture. "No, not yet as an adult. There is one of me when I was nine years old, but that is in another room. I'm rather interested in the techniques of capturing images on paper using light sensitive paper. Maybe I shall have one of those done instead. But then, portraits are often done with a little artistic licence. Especially if the subject is not quite so beautiful as they should be."

"You will have no need for such licence then," Boyd said, then added, "The servant told us the ornamental gardens were your father's design."

"Yes. He liked things ordered. I prefer something less structured, more natural. But I maintain that section of the garden as he liked it, in his memory. I've always thought of myself not as the owner of this estate, but as the custodian for future generations."

Boyd nodded, and a short time later, a servant entered.

"Ma'am, there is Mr Francis outside. He hopes to speak to you about Miss Potts."

"Mr Francis?"

Charles noticed her surprised reaction and tried to guess why. Who was this man and why he was calling on her?

"Yes." The servant awaited the instructions.

"I shall come and speak to him." Then addressing the

three visitors, "Would you excuse me for a few moments? I must speak to Mr Francis." She was aware that she was probably being rude by leaving them, but she didn't care. She didn't care if he thought her discourteous.

Mr Francis stood outside the drawing room in the hallway. Louise approached him and shook his hand.

"Mr Francis, I'm sorry I cannot invite you in properly, but I have business acquaintances visiting at the moment."

"It is I who should beg your pardon. I didn't wish to disturb you. I shall return at a more convenient time." He turned to go, but she stopped him.

"No, no we can speak now. I just can't invite you in. You wanted to know about Lu- Miss Potts?"

A broad smile spread across his face. "Yes. I wished to speak to her. I have returned from Manchester to see her. I have obtained a position with a reputable firm." He blushed as he spoke. "And I wished to speak to her, only to find she has returned to Bedfordshire."

Louise guessed what he wanted to speak about, and she sensed he knew it too. It pleased her that she was indeed right in her advice to Lucy that Mr Francis had waited to obtain a position before he made her an offer of his hand. But mostly she was happy for the pair. Although she had seen little of them together, she knew enough of them separately to know that they were very much in love. Lucy in her three months of silent brooding, Mr Francis in his deep blush and awkwardness just now when Lucy's name was mentioned.

"Unfortunately, yes, she has returned to Bedfordshire," Louise said. "But I'm sure if you were to stop there on your way back to Manchester you would find a cordial welcome from her parents. Although I haven't met them, Lucy assures me that they are very agreeable."

"Was she well when you left her?"

"Yes, perfectly, although a little sorry to return to England. She thoroughly enjoyed her time in Paris. As did I. She was a perfect traveling companion, insisted we went to places that I never would have thought of, or would have considered, much to my own enjoyment. Mr Francis, would your grandparents think it reproachful if I asked you to dine here tonight? They wouldn't miss you for one evening?"

"Why thank you, yes." Astonishment spread on his face. "It would be an honour. I'm sure my grandparents will be more than happy for me to attend."

"The honour is mine; in fact, you would be doing me a great service. The businessmen I'm in conference with at the moment shall be dining here too, and I have the feeling that they only accepted out of obligation. It would be most advantageous for me to have a friend at the table."

The thought that Mr Francis had also accepted out of duty didn't cross her mind. But she needn't have worried, an invitation from such an eminent person was something Mr Francis had never before received. He had heard, like many others, that she kept an excellent table.

"I shall send a carriage for you at seven."

"But Miss Thomas, that is too much!"

"Nonsense. I know your grandparents have no horse. I couldn't invite you, then expect you to walk."

. . .

When the three gentlemen arrived back at the inn later that afternoon, Mr Ashton was in a jovial mood. Having secured the funding and having met with Robert Adams, there was little that could dampen his spirits.

They were about to adjourn to their separate rooms to prepare for dinner when they were called into the tap room by the landlord, who inquired if they would need their supper. He was a rather gruff-looking old man, who had obviously seen a fight or two, because of his crooked nose.

It was Ashton who replied. "No, thank you. We're to dine at Glazebrook House tonight."

The landlord's eyebrows raised up in surprise. "You'll eat the best food then. Miss Thomas is said to serve her guests only the finest."

"Indeed!" Ashton said, and decided to try and obtain more information. "Tell me, is Miss Thomas well-liked in the area?"

"Yes, she's liked. Has people queuing up to work for her. She pays well and even pays the doctor's fees for her staff, should they need him. She knows the name of all her tenants, and her staff."

All three men listened intently. The landlord continued in a soft West Country accent: "She's a worthy trustee of the estate and is kind to the poor. Yes, she's well liked. Nothing much to dislike about her. Folk round here worry who she might marry though."

"What do you mean?"

"People fear she'll come back from one of her trips to London engaged to some worthless fellow. So far, we've been lucky. But it will happen one day, I'm sure. Then we'll be in trouble." He wiped the counter with a cloth, even though it was already spotlessly clean.

"I've heard she's somewhat eccentric?" Ashton asked.

"She is a little. The very rich often are, although I think her only really strange way is that she rides her horse like a man: astride and with trousers on. I've seen her several times too. A great horsewoman she is, as good as any man. A strange sight it is though. Some people say she rides bareback too, but I've never seen it.

"Her old governess Miss Gately that was, lives up yonder.

Says she was a lovely child and hasn't a bad word to say about her. Says Miss Thomas thinks every child from every background should be taught to read and write and given an education. Not sure I agree with that. She started the school up the way and pays for it all though she don't boast about it. Every job available at her estate has at least ten people wanting it, not that there are many going. Nobody leaves a good employer such as her unless it's in a wooden box. Not put her rent up for five years. Not like Sir Giles – he's a bad 'un. No, you'll not hear a bad word against her."

"Rides her horse like a man!" Ashton laughed. "I must remember that tonight as we're sitting at dinner."

But Charles didn't share his humour. He wouldn't laugh at her. He had seen a side to her today that he never knew existed; she was guardian to so much, bore so much responsibility by herself. He mulled over her words; not spoken so that he could hear, but heard all the same as she said them to Mr Boyd while they looked at her parents' portraits:

"I do not consider myself the owner of all this, I'm simply the custodian for future generations."

If he had accepted her offer of marriage, then perhaps he would be the one deciding where the money to invest was to go. He never had any problem getting funds for anything he designed, especially in these recent years as his reputation as a master engineer grew. What would he do with such a large amount of money? He knew; he would give it back to her. She must lead a lonely life, for although she had many grateful servants and tenants, at the end of each day, as they went to their quarters or houses, she was alone. He started to see why she craved family life so.

No, he wouldn't laugh at her. Circumstances beyond her control had carved her characteristics, and without her father to guide her. It was no wonder she had strange opinions and habits. But he realised now that she could no more walk away from this responsibility she had been born into than he could walk away from his engineering.

He started to regret even more the way he had spoken to her that day – how he had chided her, how he had put her down! He was determined tonight he must at least speak to her again, to try to make further amends. If not for his own conscience, then for Jane's.

15

As Louise dressed that evening, she could hardly have known all her guests were eager to attend. She assumed they had accepted her invitation out of obligation, but she couldn't have known that all of them had a keenness to speak to her at length over dinner. Despite knowing her position in life was elevated above many, she never believed herself above those gentlemen who were at the pinnacle of the industrial world. As for Mr Francis, she was sure he would soon be her friend's husband, and for that alone, he deserved her civility. She descended the great staircase at Glazebrook and trembled a little at the thought that yet again, Mr Lucas was to be in her home. This led her to check and double check every arrangement to the point where her normally patient servants grew exasperated. It was only when the clock struck seven thirty that she took a sip of wine for courage, and waited for the sound of the carriages that would herald their arrival.

She often gave dinners for friends and acquaintances, but generally preferred to eat the more plain food that was served for the servants on those nights when she was alone. Her cook, the best in Devon, thought this very irregular, but followed her orders and simply prepared her mistress's food with the utmost care and attention. Despite her position as mistress, she didn't believe it worth the effort for the cook to prepare delicate dishes for only one person. So, on such occasions as these, the servants were more than obliging to make extra effort for their most highly regarded employer.

The guests arrived in their separate carriages only a few minutes late. They stepped out and their host awaited them in the sitting room. It was warmed by a blazing fire and lit by many candles.

The introductions were made. "You are Charles Lucas?" Mr Francis said after a moment, with eyes wide. "The famous engineer?"

"Yes," Charles said in reply, not flinching from Mr Francis's reaction. Louise watched on, a little amused. Had she also been so obviously in awe all those months ago when she first met him?

Soon enough they all found themselves seated for dinner in the grand dining room. Mr Ashton and Mr Francis were seated either side of her at the head of the table. Mr Lucas, and Mr Boyd were furthest away, but since the table could seat twenty people, they all sat at one end. Louise's gaze went over the spread. Everything was just as she had arranged it – the best silver and dinner service and her finest crystal glasses all added to the finery and opulence. She was determined to give them a taste of elegance – to give him an idea of what he had rejected. He might not like her class and wealth, but she wouldn't hide what she had. Why should she?

As they ate, the conversation took many turns and eventually went to the Glazebrook estate.

"I hear you have a palm house, Miss Thomas," Ashton commented.

"Yes, it was built in 1823, as a wedding gift from my father to my mother. She was fond of tropical plants."

"A palm house. That is a rarity," Boyd said.

"It was designed by Decimus Burton. One of his first," she stated.

"Really? And have you seen his new palm house at Kew?" Ashton asked.

"Yes. I was invited to the opening a few years ago. He remembered my father and his early commission of work and wanted a representative to be there."

"A palm house is an extravagant gift. The window tax alone must have been a great burden." Charles asked.

"It was, but I couldn't bear to have it torn down. My mother loved it more than any other place on the estate. Besides, it is not an issue now that window tax has been repealed, much to my great relief. Although I'm sure the government will find a different way to tax me."

"Tell me, what is that big stone that sits near the gatehouse, the one that sits on the knoll. It looks a little odd there, a bit out of place." Charles asked, eager to have her speak to him again.

"You mean the Dancing Stone?"

"The Dancing Stone? A stone that dances?" His brow raised in amusement.

"Do tell the story Miss Thomas," Mr Francis interjected eagerly. "I'm sure they will find it interesting."

"Perhaps," she said. "But only if you like to hear a little mythology. A stone that is said to dance is no scientific fact."

Charles nodded, and she continued. "No one knows how the stone got there and I've certainly never seen it dance. It has always been there, as far as anyone can remember. The story is that many years ago a young maiden was betrothed to a man who had to go away and fight in a war. She longed for her love to return, and would go to the knoll in order to listen out for the church bells ringing the return of the men. One of the times she was listening out a witch is said to have passed by and, seeing the love within her, grew angry at her purity and turned her into the stone. When the church bells ring, the stone is said to dance because it holds the soul of the maid. She thinks she will see her betrothed again."

"A fanciful story for a stone! Do you believe the stone dances?" Boyd asked her.

They all stared at her and awaited her response.

"Certainly not. But it gives me something to talk about when I have guests to dinner," she said with a smile.

"Are there many other stories like this?" Charles asked.

"Do tell them about the 'Lady of the Lake'." Mr Francis said, "It's the best story around here."

"The Lady of the Lake. It sounds very mystical, do tell us," Ashton said.

Louise shook her head. "It is all folklore and fairytale." She looked about, but none of the guests seemed worried. She sighed. "Very well. There is a lake beyond the gardens here on the estate. Some people are said to have seen the ghost of a young woman float above the water, always at dusk or dawn when the mist settles a little. She is said to have been one of my ancestors who fell in love with a man who didn't return her sentiments. The gentleman in question married someone else, and the woman, believing she couldn't live without the love of this man, sewed stones into her dress, walked out into the lake and drowned herself."

"These stories often are based around unrequited love are, they not?" Mr Ashton commented.

"More often than not, yes," she replied.

"Have you ever seen the Lady of the Lake"? he asked, and expected her to answer in a similar way as before.

"No, she only shows herself to men. Legend has it that if a man looks her in the eye, she mesmerises him and lures him into the lake to drown as revenge."

Mr Ashton laughed in a nervous manner. "Well, if I visit the lake, I shall be sure to take a woman with me. I hope not all of your family are as vengeful as her?"

She looked across at Mr Lucas. "Certainly not. I'm sure that if I ever fell in love and was rejected thus, I would quickly forget the gentleman and look to the future." Charles met her gaze at first, then looked down at his plate as she finished.

But as soon as the words were out, she instantly regretted them. So far that evening she had been struggling with her composure and all day her feelings undulated from love to dislike where Mr Lucas was concerned. She was still in love with him, that she knew. She savoured being in his presence, but wanted more than anything to forget that dreadful day when he told her what he thought of her. Despite the fact that he was there that evening out of duty, he was gentlemanly and friendly. She concluded it must be because of the investments, then disliked him for his fickleness.

A short time later, Mr Boyd asked, "Whilst Charles and I walked out this afternoon, we were caught in a shower and made our way to a small outbuilding beyond the stables. At first we assumed it was a farm building, but when we went in, it wasn't full of animals, it was full of strange objects. There were miniature steam engines, chemical experiments of kinds and image-taking equipment, and in it there was a desk with all sorts of journals, including the Engineering

Journal, and there was even a sketch of Charles's bridge on the wall."

Louise froze, overcome with horror at their discovery of her workroom.

Mr Boyd went on, "Do you know who the workroom belongs to? I would like to direct him, whoever he is. Is he one of your servants? Many of the experiments were quite elementary. But perhaps it's set up to teach a child?"

Everyone looked at Louise for a response. She cleared her throat and looked over at Mr Lucas. From the look on his face, he obviously knew the truth. He had been here all this time and he knew her secret. Boyd's condescension made it impossible for her to admit to being the owner. Finally, he glanced at her and must have seen the mortification and embarrassment on her face.

At last she spoke, but the words were difficult to find. "I – I will make sure the owner of the workroom knows of your views," she said, and she dipped her head in shame, suddenly wishing the visitors were gone.

She barely heard Mr Lucas speak, but it was his voice that made her look up. "Miss Thomas, you were right about being able to see Portland from the coastline. I have never been there, have you?"

She lowered her voice. "Yes. Many times. I'm fond of Weymouth and Portland. The naval port is very fine."

"As fine as Charles's docks at Bristol?" Ashton asked.

And so the conversation finally changed to Mr Lucas's work. Louise remained somewhat quiet and subdued for the rest of the evening and barely spoke at all to Mr Boyd. She wasn't the kind of patron who was easily flattered by meaningless and unfounded compliments, so Mr Boyd's remarks, although truthful, would normally have been accepted with fortitude. But she was in no mood for further criticism, especially tonight, and because her workroom was her most favourite place in the whole of her estate. The invasion, however inadvertent, into this most private place had wounded her deeply and she didn't know if she could find the courage to speak to Mr Boyd without her sudden dislike showing. She would make sure she always locked the place from now on and was the only key holder. Why hadn't she done that before?

When dinner was over, Louise stood up to leave the men alone.

Ashton was the first to protest. "No! Miss Thomas, there is no need to leave us. You're the only lady and our host, surely you need not stand on such ceremony?"

But she was determined. "I'm sorry, I must insist. I wouldn't like you all to think me more male than female." She shot a glance at Mr Lucas, but scolded herself for her pettiness. She lightened her tone. "Please join me in the sitting room when you are ready. You know where it is."

The gentlemen remained in the dining room only a quarter of an hour. Their conversation was somewhat limited. Mr Lucas was no longer in the mood for idle chit-chat, Mr Francis was too awed to say much and Mr Boyd and Mr Ashton had no subject to speak of except the dinner, and the dining room in which they sat.

Louise used the time alone to visit the kitchens to thank the staff. It was a custom she kept after her guests left, but the thought of being alone for an unknown amount of time in the sitting room was almost unbearable. She was back in her place ready to serve the coffee as soon as the gentlemen entered. She had spent the previous minutes lingering on why she couldn't be in the same room as Mr Lucas without being mortified and humiliated. Wasn't it enough that he disliked her?

Luckily, the rest of the evening passed with little incident. Conversation remained pleasant enough. Mr Ashton claimed a desire to see the house and grounds more fully the next time he was in Devon. When the carriages were called for, Mr Lucas cornered her and asked if she would grant a moment of her time to speak to him in private.

She agreed, ignoring the surprised and inquisitive looks from the others. She led him to the drawing room, entering in only a few paces. Only when she heard the door close did she dare look at him. She half expected his criticism and chastisement. She expected him to launch into a tirade like the last time they spoke alone, to tell her the things he hated about her house, her behaviour.

He cleared his throat and hesitated for a moment, then in a quiet, sincere voice began. "Firstly, I would like to apologise for Mr Boyd's earlier comments about your workroom. I know him well enough to assure you that he didn't mean anything malicious."

She tilted her chin up at him and said in proud defiance, "You need not worry, Mr Lucas. I will not change my mind about funding the bridge because of Mr Boyd's comments, however deep they cut. The percentage of the toll charges I will receive will be a useful income for the estate for many years. Besides, this is different from the usual slights I receive, most of which are aimed at my character and reputation rather than my personal interests."

What could he say in return? He deserved that remark and, looking at her wounded expression, he was at a loss for words for a moment. "You mistake me. I wasn't apologising for him in order to secure the investment, I assure you. It was because I knew he had offended you."

"And may I ask why you so suddenly care if I'm offended

or not, having given me such thorough admonishment before?"

He couldn't answer that question either. She had caught him off guard.

"Miss Thomas please, I'm truly sorry for our misunderstanding that day. For my foolishness in believing Mr Risinger. Can you find it in yourself to forgive me?"

She held his gaze for a long time. "Yes."

He sighed, then moved closer to her. "Thank you. Though I know I don't deserve it. Believe me, Jane has made me suffer most acutely for my error."

"Mr Russell visited you then?"

"He did."

She looked down for a moment. "William – Mr Risinger deceived you, in the same way he deceived me. He has a manner and demeanour that appears to make him trustworthy, but rest assured – underneath is a fiend."

"I know."

"He charmed me, he is handsome and has such a way with words that some days I still wonder to myself that he did all this. What pains me the most is if he had been inclined to be kind and generous there would have been a great many people who would have benefited from him. But alas, he chose a different path."

"You were great friends before his deception?"

"Yes, I looked on him as a brother. But all he wanted was my money and my estate. God knows what he would have done with it."

Charles noticed how sad her face had become. "Worst of it all was to claim that Marie was your child, when all along – "

Louise interrupted him. "That he claims the child is mine proves once and for all that he does not know me. For

I could never abandon a child, however unfortunate the circumstances may have been regarding its birth. I have so few blood relatives that I would cherish any God blessed me with."

She took a breath, then continued on in a passionate tone. "I have independence and can act in any way I choose. If I had wanted to, I could have followed the immoral path, and not answered to anyone. But I have not."

"I know." He paused, staring at her for a moment. "Tell me, has he been found yet?" He hoped his voice showed genuine concern.

"No, he still hides himself away. He is so much in debt and with such unsavoury people that he fears too much for his life. Who can possibly be hiding him, I know not."

"Is everything being done to find him?"

"Mr Russell assures me that it is."

"And is the child safe?"

"Yes, quite safe. She is in a village just north of Nottingham. So, you see, you need not worry on that score. I'm sure eventually Mr Risinger will be found, dead or alive. I no longer care which."

Silence ensued for a few moments. Every subject now seemed exhausted. But there was one further matter he must speak of.

"Can I ask you, would you receive a letter from Jane? She would like to renew her friendship with you."

The mention of such a treasured friend softened her demeanour. "Oh Jane. How is she? I miss her very much. Yes, tell her I would be so glad to hear from her."

"Thank you. She is well. She will be happy to hear from you. Although I'm not sure what I shall say regarding the reason for my visit."

"Tell her the truth – tell her my secret. She loves you and

Mr Boyd too much to disclose my secret and risk harming both your livelihoods."

She hadn't meant to be so indiscreet on Jane's part, but the look of surprise on Mr Lucas's face was clear. He hadn't realised that his sister's friendship with Miss Thomas was such that she would discuss Mr Boyd. No wonder Jane had been so upset – their friendship ran deeper than he ever realised.

"I'm sorry. I should not have made that last comment about Mr Boyd," she said.

He dismissed the remark, and walked towards her. "Will you shake my hand to show you have no ill will against me now, that you accept my unequivocal apology? I would like us to part without animosity, and perhaps if you're willing, start afresh?"

She was a little taken aback but took his hand for a moment. Something deep within her couldn't deny him anything he asked. "Certainly. But will you be so kind as to inform Mr Boyd that in the future it would be preferable that he keep his admonishments of those intellectually beneath him to himself."

"I will."

With that, he let her smaller hand slip out of his and they returned to the other guests. It was a few minutes more before the carriages arrived and they took their leave.

. . .

As the carriage returned them to the inn, Charles was quiet. He still felt his apology was lacking. But he was glad to get away; it was all awkward to say the least. It was clear she didn't want to be in his company, but then why invite him to dinner?

He was at least glad that Jane would no longer complain

at the loss of her friend. He was determined to write to her immediately and tell her the news.

But the workroom had unsettled him. Ever since he had been inside it, he had been unable to stop thinking about it. That room with all its technology showed that she had more than a passing interest in such things, that she filled her time with all that interested him. She was different to other women, and he admired her for it.

He thought back to her question. Why do you so suddenly care if I'm offended or not? His heart whispered one reason, but he quickly suppressed it.

. . .

After Louise bid farewell to her guests, she went to the dining room, now clear of all signs of the gathering. She sat down quietly on the chair Mr Lucas had occupied, trying to hold on to his essence, and at the same time thinking of the touch of his hand a few minutes earlier.

She was angry at herself for allowing her emotions to show and overflow into words directed at him. She had been petty at times, but she knew that it was precisely because she loved him so, that she cared what he thought of her, that he was able to bring forth such emotions. Why did he still have such an effect on her? She was glad to know that at least he thought a little better of her. He admitted to being wrong over Mr Risinger. But she couldn't help wishing his feelings were as deep as hers. In fact, hadn't his apology been solely directed towards his error, and not those personal faults he clearly pointed out that day?

The evening had been full of emotional turmoil and she abruptly stood up and removed herself from the dining room, in a determined effort to forget him. She couldn't continue to brood over him like this. He didn't like her and she was resolved to overcome her feelings once and for all.

The first step was to occupy her mind with other things, and she spent the remainder of the night writing to Jane. She couldn't wait for Jane to contact her, she had permission from the brother to renew their friendship and she wouldn't delay any longer. The previous three months had been long enough.

16

—————

The partners left Axminster the next morning for their journey to the bridge construction site. Charles woke in an unhappy mood. He hadn't slept well, and whether this was because of the general noise from the inn or from the torrent of thoughts that invaded his mind, he didn't know. All he knew was that he was unsettled. They sat in the first class carriage and waited for the train to leave the station. Ashton took up a newspaper and Mr Boyd a book. But Charles wasn't about to let the other two read. He had business to discuss.

"Before you both spend the entire journey reading, I have something I wish to say to you."

Ashton peered over his newspaper and Boyd closed his book.

"Go ahead," Boyd said.

"Firstly, Ashton: never again will you take me somewhere without telling me first where we're going and whom we are to meet."

Ashton grunted when he saw the serious look on Charles's face and shrugged one shoulder. "As you wish."

Charles continued, "I'm aware that as part of my job in this partnership, I must meet with people I do not like and be civil and affable to them, and I'm prepared to do that if you ask me. But I want advance warning."

"Quite so. I'll not do it again. But just you remember your promise just now. I won't have you complaining, especially if you have to meet with Robert Adams again."

"I can promise you, I will never complain at meeting Robert Adams again, or anyone else."

"Is that all?" Ashton asked.

"For you, yes."

Ashton opened his newspaper again and safely placed himself behind it.

Charles turned to Boyd, who wondered what his admonishment could be. He watched Charles as he took a deep breath and tried to find the words.

"Yesterday at dinner you deeply offended Miss Thomas. I'm surprised she didn't pull out of the bridge investment there and then."

Boyd frowned, then his mouth opened and he went red. "What did I say?"

Ashton placed his newspaper down. "Tell me she has not changed her mind?"

"No, when I spoke to her last night, she said she would honour the promise. But that is not the point," Charles said, then turned again to Boyd. "The workroom you described as elementary belongs to Robert Adams."

Boyd closed his mouth and opened it again. "But she is Robert Adams!"

"Exactly. They are her experiments, her miniature engines, her desk with journals, and she sketched the bridge at the lecture I gave in London all those months ago."

He felt a little odd admonishing Boyd for a small misdemeanour when he himself had done far worse to her. But he was unexpectedly overcome with emotion. He wanted to protect her, to make the pain he and Boyd had caused go away. His thoughts were interrupted by Ashton as he tutted and said to Boyd. "Remind me to keep you away from our investors in the future."

"Her room?" Boyd said in a strangled tone.

"Yes. I know enough of her to know that she is unconventional, and that she takes an interest in those things normally reserved for men. I realise it was furthest from your mind that the room was hers. But hers it was and is. She asked me to tell you to not make jest of those who are not as intelligent as yourself."

Boyd pulled at his shirt collar. "But, I have to say, I have never thought she lacked intelligence. Quite the opposite in fact."

"Nor I," Charles was proud to say.

After a pause, Ashton asked with raised eyebrows and a sarcastic tone. "By the way Charles, why was Miss Thomas returning your letters?"

He was spared from answering by the door to the carriage being opened and two elderly ladies entering.

"May we sit here?" one of them asked.

"Of course, please sit down." Charles indicated the seats next to him. The two women fussed around a bit and placed their bags beside them. Finally, after they settled, one of them sighed and looked around the carriage.

"First class! My my, I can't remember the last time I travelled first class."

"Me neither," the friend answered, nodding and smiling.

"It was Miss Thomas's doing of course. I told her I had to go to Exeter and when she found out my ticket was second class, she absolutely insisted on paying for my upgrade. 'My dear', she said, 'I know you have been suffering with a painful back these last few months, and those seats in second class will cause you further discomfort. I cannot hear of you travelling second class.' That is exactly what she said. She's so very kind to me, always has been. So thoughtful. Did you know she was in Paris recently with my niece Lucy?"

The friend nodded.

"Lucy wrote to me last week, and told me of their trip, and said that Miss Thomas received three offers of marriage while she was there." She waved her hand about. "All fortune hunters of course. I'm sure if she ever received an offer from a gentleman who she knew truly loved her she would accept at once, but while she has such a large fortune she can never be sure of a man's true sentiments. It's such a shame she isn't married, she deserves someone to look after her for a change. But I'm not sure such a gentleman exists."

The woman leaned forward and whispered loudly. "She told Lucy once that she has received seven offers of marriage all together, not including the ones in Paris, and refused them all!"

"Really? Seven?" her friend said.

"Yes, but with those other three in Paris, that makes ten. It's not that unusual though considering what a worthy woman she is. She was a lovely child. I remember when she was born. Her mother loved her so! Always wanted a daughter. Never spoiled her, but always made sure she knew her duty. It's no surprise she turned out so well. Sir Robert was an excellent father too." The lady sighed again. "It's such a shame she's all on her own in that big house. It isn't fair that she should have nobody to turn to in times of trouble. Of course, I believe she has one friend, her cousin Lord Philip Eldon. He has been a great companion to Miss Thomas,

Lucy told me. She said Miss Thomas always speaks fondly of him. It was his apartment they stayed in at Paris. I wonder whether he might do for her? I hear his estate in Northumberland is twice the size of Glazebrook, so all the advantage would be on her side. But then, we wouldn't see her often if she was all that way north! No, better she marry someone more local! But who?"

Charles looked out of the window and listened with frustrated calmness. Was there nowhere he could escape her? His head was still full of her, and he had hoped that after speaking to his partners he could finally put her out of his mind and concentrate on the task at hand. But the words of praise were not in vain. Mr Boyd started to feel he had done a great deal of harm to such a kind person, and wondered if he should ever be allowed to speak to investors again. Mr Ashton, still amused at the image of Miss Thomas riding her horse like a man, thought it all rather amusing that two ladies would talk about the marriage prospects of their patron in a public place and for anyone to overhear.

. . .

A few days later, in London, Jane received her letter from Louise and set about replying as soon as she could.

My dearest Louise

I cannot tell you how overjoyed I was to receive your letter. It was such a delight – so unexpected and what I have desired for the last two months. I was in raptures for hours afterwards, Mother will testify to that. I could think of nothing else for some time.

I'm glad you didn't wait for Charles to write to me first. He can be such a lazy correspondent at times that Mother and I despair of him. He always keeps in touch when he is away but his letters are rushed and not informative. Mother sends her love to you. She is anxious to see you and was as happy as I when she heard you had written.

After Charles's previous behaviour I wouldn't have blamed you at all if you washed your hands of us Lucases completely. But you're so forgiving and I'm glad but not surprised. Charles takes his role in looking after me so seriously, but fails to realise that most of the time I can look after myself. He does mean well, however. Not that it as any excuse for what he did. If only he listened to Mother and I none of this nasty business would ever have happened.

Mother wishes Charles would marry and then he will have a wife to fuss over and leave his sister alone. But I should not complain. Despite his inability to judge character he does what he thinks best, and one of my friends, Mary, her brother is such a tyrant to her, I don't know how she copes.

I'm rambling now, forgive me, and I normally write such well thought out letters.

I would love to know all about your time in Paris and I can assure you I wouldn't think it dull as you stated. I have been to France twice, but never Paris. Is it very much like London?

The letter continued on for two more pages, full with news from London – what was playing, who was in town.

When Jane walked out to post her letter, she arrived back to find her Mother had awoken from her afternoon sleep.

"Jane dear, were you out?"

"Yes Mother, I posted my letter to Louise."

"I'm glad you were quick in replying. She will know how much you treasure her friendship. Tell me, what did you say?"

"Nothing of great interest, just that she should never mind Charles if he does such a thing again, and that we think he should marry so he can fuss over his wife and not me!"

"Indeed Jane. Did you say anything about who Charles should marry?" Mrs Lucas asked. Jane sat next to her.

"No. Why would I? I'm sure Charles will never marry. He's too disinterested in ladies and spends far too much time working."

"You didn't say that in your letter did you?"

"No, why?"

"It's just that, well . . ." Mrs Lucas paused as her daughter looked inquiringly at her. "You know I love Charles as much as any woman loves her son, and I want him to be happy. But sometimes he doesn't know what is in front of him."

"What are you trying to say?"

"I had rather hoped before all this nastiness with Miss Thomas, that she and Charles would marry."

Jane sat open-mouthed.

"Don't tell me you've never thought of it!" her mother scoffed.

"No! Yes, I mean. No."

"You wouldn't like Charles to have such a wife? Wouldn't you like to have your friend as a sister?"

"Yes, of course. But Charles certainly has never looked upon her with admiration, and as for her, do you think such a woman would wish to marry Charles, especially after his past behaviour?"

"I don't know about Charles, but does he have to admire her in order to marry her? As for Miss Thomas, well Jane, I have been in this world long enough to recognise when a lady is in love."

"Louise – love Charles?" Jane said incredulously.

"I believe so, yes."

"Has she ever said anything to you?"

Her mother was silent for a few moments, thinking back to the time at the assembly months ago. Should she say anything?

Jane's reaction to her mother's silence was immediate. "She did say something! What did she say? Did she say she loved Charles?"

"No, not exactly, but she didn't have to. Every time the two of them met ... think about it Jane; her eyes were always on him, her cheeks were always slightly flushed and there was something in her eye. Oh, as I sit here now I can see her face the moment he walked into the assembly room that night. It was as though a fire was ignited within her. She didn't say anything directly, only commented that Miss Hunter appeared to admire Charles. I simply replied that Miss Hunter was the furthest in my mind as a suitable match, that we would all wish for a more deserving wife for him."

"But I didn't notice her admiration. How can you be sure?"

"You simply weren't looking. As I said my dear child, I know when a woman is in love."

"It's incredible."

"It's not incredible that any woman should love my dear Charles."

"No, but I can't believe I didn't see it."

This revelation caused all sorts of questions in Jane's mind. Was it really true that Louise could love her brother? Was he the man she had spoken about having feelings for? If she did love him, then his admonishment would have made her pain even more acute. Could she still love him after what he did? Jane thought about the two of them marrying. It would certainly be to great advantage for Charles, but he wouldn't be so mercenary. Louise was fast becoming a dear friend. A dear friend whom she valued greatly.

But no, it would never happen. Charles wasn't an admirer of the gentry. He had always believed them greedy and lazy. His prejudice was too great to overcome.

Eventually Jane spoke. "Mother, I think you're misleading yourself if you think such a match will happen. I know you want him to marry well but after everything that has happened I cannot see how it could take place."

"Oh Jane! Give it time. Already they have started to make amends. Didn't Miss Thomas say that Charles had visited her and apologised and she had forgiven him? Give it time, Jane. We shall see the two in mutual happiness, I'm sure."

. . .

In Plymouth, work on the bridge temporarily banished thoughts of Miss Thomas from Charles's mind. The work progressed well, and in between the dinners given by local dignitaries and other distractions, the two weeks he spent in Devon were not too unpleasant. It was on the last two nights before his departure that he started to wish himself back in London and away from the county she lived in.

Those two nights, he was woken by separate dreams. In the first he had been walking by a lake and the ghost of a woman rose out of the water. She was beautiful, alluring, her long dark hair flowed over her naked body, but he couldn't see her face. Fully clothed, he waded out into the water. With each step, he grew more desperate to see the woman, but she hid her face as she cried. Finally, he was close enough. He reached out his hand to touch her, to stop her sobbing. He had to stop her sobbing.

He touched her arm, and she instantly looked up.

"Louise," he whispered. Suddenly he was under the

water drowning; desperate for air, he could feel himself suffocating.

He woke himself up, sweat dripping from him.

The second night wasn't much better. This time, he was at dinner with Miss Thomas, much in the same way as he had been nearly two weeks before. William Risinger entered the room and grabbed her. He struck her once, then laughed and struck her again and again. Charles tried to stop him, he tried to get to her, but he couldn't. He was paralysed. Risinger was laughing, Miss Thomas was screaming, and again he woke sweating.

It took him hours to get back to sleep both nights. Was this her punishment to him? To haunt his dreams? The thought of Risinger striking Miss Thomas had never before affected him so. He wished she had never been subject to such terrible behaviour. How he despised Risinger. To do such a thing to a woman. If she were his sister he would have made sure he paid. But she wasn't. She acted as she saw fit and answered to no one.

Everyone he met who knew Miss Thomas spoke so well of her. How could he have been so blind to her good qualities? Then, he remembered her forgiveness. She shook his hand that night, despite having every right to refuse.

But it was the workroom that was his undoing. Yet again he thought back to the contents of that room. He imagined her there at all hours, as she worked on experiments, watched the miniature engines, read journals, studied to further her mind. Reading his articles – she admitted to that herself. He liked the thought of her reading his work. It somehow made him feel closer to her, however strange it was.

Then there was the train journey from Axminster, and the old lady on the train. Did she always do such kind things to those who lived on her estate? He imagined her going around helping anyone she could. She did have a generous heart. She was unusual and independent and at first he had been unsettled by it. But now all he could do was admire her. All other women seemed ordinary compared to her.

17

————

The day Lucas, Ashton and Boyd departed from Axminster, Louise busied herself with estate matters, but on more than one occasion looked at the clock and wondered if they had gone yet, or if something could have delayed them.

"Surely they would have caught the 9.56 train to Exeter, because any later train would make the connection to Plymouth extremely vexing," she told herself.

By the afternoon she had convinced herself that they must have left and went for a lonely walk to the coast to try to come to terms with her feelings, only to remember as she passed her workroom that this was the walk that Mr Lucas had taken the day before.

She entered the workroom and looked around the place she knew so well. She suddenly recalled Mr Boyd's comments, and with an angry sweep of her hand knocked her engine models to the ground. She went across to another bench and smashed each chemical container one by one. There! She would never again have to endure such humiliation. Without a care for the shards of glass that littered the floor, she crouched down in front of the fireplace and struck match after match until the coals were properly aflame. Hot tears of self-pity and frustration rolled down her cheeks – she couldn't even light a fire competently!

"I shall always be a child to such men," she thought sadly as she burnt each volume of the journals, and her painstaking notes.

She resolved to never see any of them again, in particular Mr Lucas. She would make sure that when in London, Jane would visit her and she would go out of her way to avoid him. What annoyed her most was that he had only apologised because of the revenue they were going to receive. She couldn't bear it that he was like those other men who courted her because of her money. Curse her money! Curse her estate! It was a millstone around her neck, pulling her down into an abyss of endless loneliness. She would much rather be poor and happy with a large family to cherish her and she them.

She watched the flames for a while, then stood up and saw on the wall the sketch of his bridge design. She reached out to rip it off, but her hand paused. She couldn't bring herself to burn it. She had drawn it that first day she had met him at the lecture, when he was so amiable. She had sat drinking in everything he said as he spoke to the crowded lecture hall. She remembered the smile on his face while she asked him awkward questions.

"Why could you not love me?" she said aloud.

No, she couldn't burn that memory, however much pain he had caused her since.

Eventually, she left the workroom and vowed never to return to it and have it razed to the ground.

She walked blindly on to the coast and sat down in her favourite spot, overlooking the sea. It was a rough day and the waves crashed in one after the other even though there was little wind. The crackle of the sea on the pebbles comforted her. There and then she decided when she returned to the house that she must do as she had said yesterday; she must get on with her life and never think about him again. She walked down to the beach and picked up a pebble, then threw it into a wave as it hit the beach.

"I wish you well, Charles Lucas," she whispered.

She picked up another. "I will always love you," she said as she threw it in. "But I can't let you control my thoughts forever."

Shortly after, with sad determination, she made her way back to her house and the responsibilities she had earlier despised. How foolish she now felt in ever having believed that a man such as Mr Lucas could love her. What was she to such a man? She had nothing except her money to attract any gentleman, and he looked for something more than privilege and status. Such stupidity to think he could like her! His angry face flashed in front of her again as she remembered his disdain at the thought of marrying her.

But now she had to walk away from such irrational thoughts with a new determination. She loved him, she would always love him, and he couldn't stop her from loving him. But she would learn to move on to a new stage of her life, one that didn't contain such romantic thoughts.

Over the subsequent weeks, she threw herself into her estate work, was an attentive neighbour and was more benevolent than ever to the poor and needy. At night, whenever she was on her own, she sat reading books that would improve her mind, as well as novels and poetry. Jane's letters came fast and frequently, but she wrote little of her brother, and when she did mention him, Louise trained her mind not to dwell on the words.

The workroom she had desecrated was left standing despite her previous vow to have it knocked down. She entered it again and tidied it. She would not let Mr Lucas or My Boyd stop her from pursuing her most favourite past time.

It wasn't many weeks before she received the letter she had expected from her friend Lucy Potts.

My dearest Miss Thomas,

I cannot contain myself, I'm happy beyond words. I think you will guess when I say what has caused such delight. I'm engaged! Mr Francis visited me yesterday most unexpectedly, saying that you of all people had told him to do so. I'm so happy I could burst! I must thank you from the bottom of my heart.

It all happened so quickly. I was busy helping my mother rearrange her chamber furniture when the maid came in and said that Mr Francis was waiting for me downstairs.

Of course, at first I didn't believe her, but she assured me it was him.

I composed myself as best I could and we sat having tea with Mother and Father, until a little later he asked if I would like to walk out to show him the village. Well, I was more than happy to, and before we had even walked five minutes he asked! It was so romantic. He said that he had wanted to propose before but couldn't face asking my father without securing a position. Afterwards he went straight to speak to him, and he gave his permission.

He is still here, staying at the inn in the village, but alas, he must leave in two days' time for Manchester. We haven't yet fixed a date, but Mr Francis said that he hoped we could be wed within six months.

I should so like it if you would attend our wedding, but I understand if you cannot. Please write back soon and let me have your congratulations. I'm longing to be called Mrs Francis.

Yours, etc.

Lucy Potts

P.S. He told me all about his dinner with you and the engineers. You're too kind for words to invite him, but it's so like you.

Louise smiled to herself. She was pleased Lucy had found happiness, but she wouldn't attend the wedding. She didn't plan to leave Devon within the six months Lucy stated and Bedfordshire was such an awkward distance that she couldn't travel for only one day. No, she was sure it was unlikely she could go. Only a few days earlier, Jane had entreated her to come to London; but again, she had had to disappoint her. Her diversions so far had worked and she was sure that, given time, she would conquer all feelings for her love.

She was interrupted by her assistant coming in with a large parcel.

"I opened it of course," he said, handing her a box. Inside was some odd looking equipment: a piece of metal, a tube and a round solid base, a sort of plate and some pipe.

There was a slip of paper inside with the name of the contraption as well as written instructions. It read,

Mr Bunsen's natural gas burner, for the use in chemical experiments to heat liquids to very high temperatures. Patent pending and due for completion 1855.

She stared at her assistant.

"I didn't order any such an item. Who sent it?"

"There was no note, but the postmark was Plymouth," the assistant replied.

There was no doubt. It had to be from Mr Boyd, by way of apology. Mr Lucas had obviously spoken to him and since Mr Lucas had been, by Jane's account, back in London for a good few weeks, she deduced it couldn't possibly be from him.

She sighed. She was still angry at Mr Boyd. She didn't know whether she should be pleased or not. But she admitted the equipment would come in useful for her experiments. She took it to the workroom herself.

. . .

A month later and Charles, back in London, was awoken in the early hours by his sister knocking loudly at his bedroom door.

"Charles. Charles, please come quick."

He got up, put on his robe and opened the door. Jane's face was white and she was shaking. "It's Mother, they cannot wake her. I think she may be d-dead."

They quickly entered their mother's bedchamber. He went straight to her and it only took a moment for him to see that she was indeed dead.

He looked at Jane, who, seeing his grave expression and shake of the head, slumped onto the floor. He held her as she sobbed uncontrollably for many minutes. It was only when the doctor arrived that she would move away.

. . .

It was a cold October evening and Charles returned from work to find his sister alone. Now, three months since their mother died, their period of mourning was drawing to a close.

"Charles, is that you?"

"Yes Jane," he said as he entered the room and saw her standing near the fire.

"It's a cold night, there will be frost. I have asked for a fire in both our chambers."

"Thank you."

Charles stood next to his sister and warmed himself. She held a letter. He looked at it with an inquisitive gaze.

"I have just been re-reading a letter I received from Miss Thomas this morning."

"Oh?" her brother replied. It was only a few minutes since he had thought of her.

"Yes. She has been most helpful in her advice in overcoming grief. It has been quite enlightening."

"Really?" he said, trying to sound nonchalant, but was more than curious about what Miss Thomas had to say.

"Shall I read to you what she advises?"

Charles consented and Jane sat down to read an extract from the letter she held.

"It took years for me to get over the death of my father. I do not wish to make you sad or worry you about your own state of mind, but you must accept that it will take you a long time to get over the death of a dear parent. I tell you this because I believe it best to be honest. In those early days, I found myself frequently crying, and dreaded attending any event, informal or formal, without my father. But I got through each one, and I think that, once I accepted he was gone, the healing began. Remember though, retreat and grieve in private if that is what you need to do. Do not suppress the thought of her, or the wish that she was still alive. I still on occasion find my mind wandering to those precious times my father and I shared, and wishing he was still there to help me and guide me. Above all, I like to think that he is watching over me, and I remember that he is with our great Saviour now, and therefore must be happy and free from those worldly burdens we still have. I promise you, one day you will wake up and the pain will be less than the day before."

Jane placed the letter down and looked at her brother.

"It's helpful, is it not?"

"Yes. Very." He replied in a quiet voice, but the thought of Louise suffering did nothing to relieve him.

"She must have had a much more difficult time than us," Jane said in a sad tone.

"What do you mean?"

"Well, only that I have you and Edward as support, but she had no-one. How lonely she must have been."

He suddenly stood up and walked to the table to get a drink. "Yes, I suppose you're right. Any loneliness we feel must pale in comparison to hers."

He then sat in an armchair by the fireplace, lost in thought, his drink untouched at his side. The reality of such isolation for any person must be a heavy weight indeed. He felt sorry that it was she of all people who had to bear such a state. A deep feeling of compassion welled up inside him. He couldn't think why he felt uneasy. Perhaps it was the chill of the night, or his own deep melancholy at the loss of his mother. But when he examined his feelings more deeply, he realised that his mother wasn't the reason.

He woke with a start a few hours later to find himself alone, with a blanket over him, the fire almost burnt out. He must have been more fatigued than usual by the day's activities.

He made his way to his bedchamber, but saw a light glowing inside his mother's room.

"Jane?" he pushed the door open.

He found his sister sat on the bed surrounded by a pile of letters. She looked up, her eyes brimming with tears. "I came in here because I missed her and found this box of letters in her cupboard."

"Who are they from?"

"Father. Most of them are dated before they were married."

He sat next to his sister on the bed and picked up a few. He scanned the contents. "Are they interesting?"

"It seems most were written when they were engaged and Father had to go and work in Scotland for a few months. They didn't allow the distance to quell their love for one another," she said.

"Oh?"

"There are several letters from Father, where he speaks of such love for her it's beautiful. No wonder she kept them. Here, read this one."

Jane handed him a letter and he read its contents.

After, he looked up at Jane, his expression inscrutable. "They really loved one another, didn't they?"

"Yes. And they are together again now." She swallowed a sob.

"Do you think we shall ever love anyone in that way?" he asked.

Jane hesitated.

"What is it?"

"I . . . I do love someone that way, Charles."

"Boyd?" He breathed out.

Jane dipped her head a little.

"It's no great surprise," Charles said. "I see I shall have to have words with him. When will he ask you to marry him?"

"He already has. We are engaged. We have been for the last few months. He asked me the night before mother died, and of course, during this time of mourning he couldn't speak to you to ask your permission, even if it's only a formality."

"He has done the right thing. He honours mother by not speaking to me before now."

"When shall I tell him to speak to you?"

"Tell him to come tomorrow. But I'm not sure I shall give my permission," he said with a smile. "I shall have to find out if his work prospects are good enough for you."

This small attempt at humour lifted the previous heaviness they shared and shortly afterwards they left their mother's room. But before they parted to go to their respective chambers, Jane suddenly said, "Mother always denied it but you were her favourite. She always had high hopes for you."

"I think I exceeded her expectations with the work I have done."

"Not just that, she hoped you would marry well too."

A querying look made Jane continue. "She said once that she hoped you would marry Miss Thomas. But we both know that will never happen. Well, good night."

"Good night," he said, closing the door to his bedroom and sitting on the bed.

Jane's words explained much of his mother's behaviour on the few occasions they had all been together with Miss Thomas. His mother had often tried to pull him into conversations she was having with her, and then there was the time at the assembly. He had noticed them talking and looking at him and, though he couldn't hear what they said, he wondered if his mother had encouraged Miss Thomas in her affections. Or led her to believe that he felt something for her in return.

No. It was absurd. His mother would never interfere in that way. All the time leading up to their argument, he had stated many times to his mother that he didn't like Miss Thomas in that way. He was sure he had.

But now, after all this time, he found he didn't dislike her. He would be happy to see her again when she was next in town. He wondered why she didn't come. She corresponded with Jane frequently, yet Jane didn't ask to visit her in Devon.

His earlier slumber in front of the fire had refreshed him

and he no longer found himself able to sleep. He had been troubled by some of the words written in the letter by his father. "You're all I think of," it had said. Well, if thinking of someone all the time meant you were in love, then he was most assuredly in love. He denied it, suppressed it, his mother's death delayed his admission. But Louise's words read out by Jane had touched him. He could imagine her voice speaking them. The crumbs that Jane provided only served to make him want to know more of what she wrote. Had she mentioned him? Was she well? When was she next to visit London? He started off downstairs intending to see if Jane had left the letter there, but then halfway down stopped and scolded himself for even thinking about reading someone else's letter. He returned to his room. The woman was making him act in an irrational way.

Sitting alone, he now realised he couldn't bear to go through life without her. So, this was what it was like to love, to passionately love someone. He wished Jane and Boyd well. She deserved happiness. Could he have his own?

But all he could think of now were her words that night at dinner: "If I ever fell in love and was rejected thus, I would quickly forget the gentleman and look to the future with the support of true friends."

And any hope that she still loved him was utterly and completely extinguished.

18

News of the engagement between Jane and Boyd reached Devon quickly. Jane hadn't told anyone of her betrothal before now. She thought it inappropriate to tell even her closest friends until Charles had been spoken to. But with her brother's permission, she announced it to all her friends and acquaintances. Louise, although not surprised at the match, decided she must forgive Mr Boyd for any previous offence for Jane's sake. They would make a handsome pair. Besides, Mr Boyd was still occasionally sending her anonymous gifts to make up for his error. That was admirable.

Edward was happy to see his sister suitably matched, and welcomed his future brother-in-law into the family. Jane didn't want to wait any longer than necessary for the marriage to take place. She was painfully aware, amidst all of the fuss that inevitably surrounded such an event, of Charles's sadness at parting with his sister so soon after the loss of his mother. However, she was mistaken that her brother's recent melancholy was due to her departure to another household. For although he would miss his sister, there was another reason. One he didn't speak about to anyone.

In the two months that led up to the wedding, he had fallen more in love with Louise Thomas than he would have ever thought possible, and all without seeing her once. His silent moods and sometimes fractious temperament had been sparked by the frustration of knowing not only that he had squandered the chance of marrying the woman he now loved so dearly, but that he had caused her so much pain.

He often found himself thinking about the time he had spoken so offensively, and the pain only subsided when he thought about those few seconds during which she took his hand in hers and declared her love. Then how forgiving she was afterwards. How he wanted to turn the clock back and have that time over again; how differently he would behave now!

He only wished there was a way he could make amends for everything he had said. His only prospect was that she was to attend Jane's wedding. All his hopes must hang on the short time he would have then. To do what, he didn't know. For he wasn't the sort of man who knew how to court a lady's attention. Famous engineer that he was, underneath that skill was just a man who couldn't fathom the opposite sex.

Any time that he found himself in a social situation, he would watch and listen to how gentlemen spoke to and courted ladies. Several times he observed suave, smooth speaking men as they deftly complimented their female companions. The response was usually fluttering eyelashes and giggles. But he wondered how he could ever contrive to say such things. It just wasn't in his nature.

Would Miss Thomas respond like that? No, she was more subtle and sensible. But he would hope he could provoke some sort of response from her.

. . .

Louise looked across the table at Mr Brunel. They were seated in the lounge area of the Institution of Civil Engineers. There was no one about, it being the weekend. Louise perched on the edge of her chair. Brunel sat back, relaxed and totally at ease. He removed the cigar from his mouth.

"It's clear to me you must replace your tenants' roofs with lead instead of thatch. That will stop the fires, or at least stop many of them. There are other materials available, but they are more expensive than lead -"

Louise interrupted him. "I'm assured that the walls of most of the houses will not take the weight of the lead. But more importantly, the master thatchers will get very upset."

Brunel shook his head. "Of course they don't want their livelihood taken away. Understandable. But change comes and they must learn to adapt. You're their mistress, they are your tenants. They are your houses. You must do what you consider to be best and they must live with it."

"It seems to be an impossible situation."

Brunel put the cigar back in his mouth and raised his eyebrows. "Indeed."

They said nothing for a few moments until Louise broke the silence. "Thank you for seeing me today, I shall think about your advice and do what I can to follow it."

He nodded. "Write to me again if you need further help."

"I will. You know me well enough to know I will."

Louise heard footsteps on the polished wooden floor behind but took no notice. Then she heard someone call her name.

"Miss Thomas?"

They both looked up. A familiar face looked back at her. He wore an inquisitive frown on his face. With her back to the entrance, she hadn't seen him arrive.

It was Charles Lucas.

She had of course prepared herself for this inevitable meeting, now that she was in London once again, but she was a little taken aback that he was so suddenly in front of her after all this time. She hadn't expected to see him for another few days – not until Jane's wedding. She composed herself, however, and let him take her hand in his outstretched one for a few moments.

"Mr Lucas. How unexpected. You know Mr Brunel?"

The two engineers acknowledged each other with a curt nod.

"It's I who should say it's unexpected to see you. But I suppose you being here is not so unlikely. Are you well, Miss Thomas?"

"Yes, very well. Thank you."

"I'm glad." He looked down at her. His face was serious. "Have you seen Jane yet?"

"No. But I will see her this afternoon. She is coming to tea and I'm eager to see her," she replied, with an air of forced coolness.

"She is longing to see you too, and glad you're here for her wedding. You do her a great honour by attending."

"Thank you."

"When did you arrive in London?"

"Yesterday."

"It was an easy journey?"

"Yes."

Brunel coughed and they both looked over at him. "If

you have no other questions for me, Louise, I will leave you two alone."

"Of course," she said.

Brunel heaved himself out of the chair, kissed Louise's hand and left. They watched him go, and then Charles turned to Louise.

"You were here to meet with him?"

"Yes. He has been helping me with some estate matters."

"Really?"

"Yes, roofing materials in the main, and some other things."

Charles's face darkened. "I'm sure his advice was excellent, but I would have been more than happy to assist you and answer any questions you may have had. I'm disappointed you didn't think of coming to me."

Louise looked away for a moment, then said boldly, "I did think of coming to you, but I thought you might find it petty."

His shoulders dropped. "Yes, I suppose you would think that, wouldn't you? But you do me an injustice – since seeing Glazebrook firsthand I now understand your worry over it. Besides, I thought that day we agreed to start afresh."

"Yes we did, but I didn't realise that also meant your views on estate matters had changed."

"They have."

"Oh," Louise said.

"Will you promise to come to me, and not Brunel, the next time you need advice?"

His gaze was fixed on her face and she felt a little odd. Brunel had helped her family for years. But this was him.

Before Louise could answer, she glimpsed Lord Philip by the doorway. "Are you ready Louise? I'm eager to get going," he said.

"Excuse me Mr Lucas, I must be going."

"Of course."

She took her leave and Lord Philip offered his arm. "You seem to have kept your composure while meeting that gentleman again. Wasn't he the one who caused you much trouble last year?" Philip asked once they were outside.

"Yes. But he has apologised and I have forgiven him. It's his sister whose wedding I'm attending."

"Ah. Of course. Nothing like a wedding to get the gossips talking about another. I try and avoid them myself these days – get too fed up with people asking me when I'm going to tie the knot."

"When are you going to marry, Philip?" she asked with a smile.

"Why, the day you accept me, Louise. And not a day sooner," he replied in jest.

"It looks like we're both going to remain unmarried then."

. . .

That evening, as soon as he arrived home, Charles enquired after Jane's afternoon visit to Miss Thomas.

Jane's face was animated. "It was wonderful to see her again. She looked so well. The Devon air seems to bring out a wonderful glow in her complexion. I'm sure she looks younger than I have ever seen her."

Charles couldn't help thinking the same. Louise was more beautiful than he remembered. "So your friendship is as strong as ever?"

"Yes. We talked for hours, I hardly know what about. But that is the great joy, time flies when I'm with her!"

"You should invite her to dinner before the wedding. There is still two weeks."

"I already did. But she does not have an evening free the

whole time. I was disappointed, but she has promised to see me during the day whenever I choose."

"You do not think it's because she wants to avoid Boyd?"

Jane paused for a moment. "No, no. I'm sure it's not that. He told me about his error. I spoke to her about it, and she was adamant that she wasn't offended and he didn't mean to be malicious. She simply said she had previous engagements that couldn't be cancelled. I didn't ask with whom; it would have been rude. Besides, it's none of my business. She told me they were all formed well before she arrived in London. If I had known I would have asked her before but I'm a little upset she didn't think about keeping an evening free for me."

Charles knew that she had been offended by Boyd's remarks, and couldn't blame her for wishing to avoid him, but it was inconvenient. For him at least. He wanted to see her too, to spend time with her. He wanted to show her how he felt about her. If earlier in the day was anything to go by, he had much work to do.

He was finding it increasingly difficult to think of anything else but her. It was unlikely that he could he see her during the day as his work kept him busy, and with the wedding approaching there were more things to occupy him in the evening.

The wedding day arrived and all the last minute details were arranged. However, it wasn't the bride who was to be the most admired, by one set of eyes at least. As Charles walked into the church with his sister, all gazes fell on Jane. Charles, who never usually took much note of a woman's gown, thought Jane was resplendent in her white satin (without too much frippery) and he was proud to lead her up the aisle. At the first chance, as he led his sister up the aisle, he surveyed the congregation, and his gaze locked onto Miss Thomas. There she was, on the left, the bride's side of the church. He could only see the back of her head, until she turned to see the bride, and her full beauty was once more for an instant shown to him. He dared not look at her for more than an instant, but it was long enough for him to wish that a different wedding was taking place.

It wasn't until after the ceremony that he was able to look upon her again. This time, he could take in her figure, and admire fully her elegant poise as she spoke easily with the other guests outside the church. She wore a becoming deep peach-coloured silk dress, just visible from under her light brown overcoat.

He resolved to dance with her in the evening. To hold her in his arms, or feel the touch of her hand against his once more. He had barely spoken to her.

The wedding breakfast was held in the nearby assembly rooms, and had been decorated with flowers and banners, making it, even to Charles's engineering mind, enchanting.

When the dancing started after the meal, he knew exactly where she was – seated amongst the elderly ladies and spinsters, those who didn't dance any more. He made his way over to her, but had to ask several of them to move out of the way in order to get to where she was. Eventually, he was in front of her. She was talking to his great aunt.

She noticed his presence and looked up at him enquiringly.

"Miss Thomas. Would you do me the honour of dancing with me?"

Her eyebrows rose in surprise. She turned to her companion, but the old lady looked away, as if trying to make herself invisible. His anxious look of enquiry melted her veneer of studied indifference and she found herself replying, "Yes."

He held out his hand to her; she took it lightly and stood up. The dance was the first waltz, and as it started he noticed that she was only a few inches shorter than he. But it was the touch of her hand once more and the feeling of holding her near that made his attempts at conversation falter. Both were overawed by the situation they found themselves in, yet neither could utter a word of their feelings.

Eventually, Charles spoke, determined to try to begin to win her. "It was a fine wedding."

"Yes. Jane is the most beautiful bride I have ever seen. She and Mr Boyd make a handsome couple. Their children will be very beautiful creatures."

"I can still keep a close eye on her and make sure she is treated well. It will be a little strange having a partner as a brother, but he will be kind to her and look after her as she deserves."

"I'm sure he will. And if he does not, he will have both of us to answer to, I'm sure."

"You're a loyal friend."

"You're a loyal brother."

Even after this conversation, there was still a certain reserve in her manner towards him, despite the passion of the speech she made. He wanted to break through to the woman he once knew, but could think of nothing to say, until he remarked, "Jane tells me you have forgiven Mr Boyd for his inappropriate comments. You have a generous nature, forgiving us both."

"Thank you, but you're wrong. It's not in my nature to forgive. It's something I was taught at an early age. Is it not one of the basic biblical principles? Forgive others, if you wish to be forgiven yourself. However hard it is."

"I cannot imagine what you could ever do that would need forgiveness." He looked down at her.

"A great many things, I assure you, although I shall not tell you what they are. But, when I forgive, I do not think that punishment should be avoided. Mr Risinger has taught me that lesson."

Suddenly his countenance became more serious. "No, and I deserve a great deal of punishment for my behaviour to you. When I think of what I said that day, you should hate me."

"Jane assured me in her letters that she had punished you enough!"

"Yes, I suppose she did."

They were silent for a while, until Charles decided to change the subject. "I took your advice, Miss Thomas, and recently published an article on the Tamar bridge in the Engineering Journal. Did you read it?"

"Why no, I-I didn't. When was it published?"

"A month ago. I'm disappointed you haven't read it. You are, after all, the reason I wrote it."

"I haven't been reading that journal of late." Louise thought of the pile of unread journals in her workroom. She had neither the time or the inclination to read that particular publication recently.

"You have lost interest?"

"No, I have been too busy interfering with my tenants' affairs to read anything," she smiled.

"I see," he said back in a low tone. "I still have other matters in which I need your forgiveness."

"Perhaps."

But he was secretly pleased. Her manner was slowly

softening and it reminded him of the conversations they had had when they first met.

"I had no idea you danced so well, Mr Lucas," she said, after an awkward pause.

"Thank you. I'm not an engineer all the time."

"You dance better than you play billiards, I feel," she said nonchalantly.

"You know about my billiards playing?"

"Ashton told me," she said, smiling up at him.

"He delights in telling everyone. But I must thank you for the compliment on my dancing ability. I assure you, most engineers do dance, but we choose our partners very carefully."

"I must admit, I prefer country dances."

"Really? Next you will be saying you prefer to dance the polka instead of the waltz!" he said, laughing, but then suddenly stopped when her expression gave away the truth of his remark.

For the rest of the dance, their conversation was stilted. Louise felt her deepest wishes once more re-surface and with determined effort tried to detach herself from the wondrous moment she longed for; being held in his arms. Speaking was the last thing she could possibly attempt now that her had mind realised what was happening.

The dance ended. As they stood awkwardly afterwards, one of the servants approached and whispered something to her.

She excused herself and walked away. He saw her go into the hall, and after a few moments couldn't stop himself from heading in that general direction. He watched her from a far corner as she spoke to a servant boy who had delivered a note to her.

She took it with a quizzical frown and opened it.

He watched as she placed her hand on her side and nearly crumpled to the floor. He rushed over to her, and the two of them helped her to a seat.

"Miss Thomas. Are you unwell?"

She looked up in shock. "Yes – no. I . . ."

"Is it bad news?"

"Yes. I must leave immediately." She turned to the servant who had brought the note. "Go directly to find Lord Philip. You must tell him to come to my house at once. Tell him it's imperative he comes and that I insist on it."

The servant nodded and left quickly.

"Miss Thomas, I do not wish to pry, but have you received bad news? Is it about Mr Risinger?" Charles asked with an urgent tone.

"Yes. The worst news." She handed him the note.

It was from Mr Russell, her lawyer.

Miss Thomas,

Prepare yourself for the gravest of news. Mr Risinger has taken the child. I do not know how he found out where she was, but he took her last night and had many hours for his escape before the discovery was made. He left a ransom note – I have it here with me, he demands twenty thousand pounds and will kill her if you do not pay, or if you contact the authorities.

I will go to your house shortly.

etc

He handed back the note. "I will come with you. You cannot travel alone, you have had too great a shock."

Louise looked incredulous. "Mr Lucas. This is your sister's wedding. Your place is with her!"

No, he thought, my place is with you. But her words rang true, even if his heart was telling him to comfort her, to help her in any way he could. He let out a sigh.

"I shall be perfectly safe travelling alone. I do it all the time," she continued.

"That is not what I meant. You should not be alone at this difficult time."

"I shall not be alone for long. My cousin Lord Philip will be with me shortly. He has never let me down in my time of need."

He knew from the determination on her face that further argument would be pointless. She was independent and capable, and he both resented and loved her for it.

"Then, if you will not let me help another way, tell me what I can do to help recover the child?"

"There is nothing you can do. Mr Russell has employed all the necessary people."

"Well, he obviously has not, because this wouldn't have happened in the first place."

This was the final straw for her. She had suppressed her emotions, trying to control them, but his last comment made her tears fall. He knelt down and took her hand. "I'm sorry. I should not have said that. I simply wish to help."

"Thank you,' she said. "I would be obliged if you would tell Jane that I have had to leave early due to urgent business."

He nodded, still holding her hand.

"And would you be so kind as to call my carriage?"

He reluctantly let go of her and returned shortly afterwards, bringing her overcoat and hat.

"Thank you," she replied, pleased with his thoughtfulness. In the panic of the moment she had completely forgotten she would need them.

He paced for a few moments as they both waited for the carriage, but it wasn't long before he determined that he wanted to be more use than a messenger and questioned her as much as he dare about the previous whereabouts of the child. For he decided that, with or without Miss Thomas's approval, he had to do all he could to help find the missing child, and capture the evil perpetrator once and for all.

As he handed her into the carriage, he swore a silent oath to help the dear woman he loved so much.

19

The journey from the wedding reception to her own house took Louise a mere blink of an eye, or so it seemed. Her fear for the child was such that she had never known. Only a few minutes before the news, she had been enjoying herself, being with friends, with him. But yet again, Mr Risinger ruined everything. These thoughts however, were quickly quietened. How could she be so selfish as to think of her own enjoyment when the child was in the hands of such a man? Her mind flashed images of him in prison, of him at her mercy. Would she show him mercy? She wasn't sure. The thought of him standing at the gallows was strangely comforting.

As the carriage pulled up, she quickly alighted, took a furtive look about the street and entered her house.

"Is Lord Philip here yet?" she asked the porter.

"Not yet, Ma'am."

"Very well, bring him straight up the moment he arrives," she replied, not giving him a further glance.

She went to the drawing room and paced the floor for several minutes. Waves of nausea made her sit down.

A few minutes later Lord Philip came in. Still with his coat and hat on, he entered the room and she flew into his arms.

Philip released her after some time and attempted to restore at least a small amount of optimism.

"Come now, Louise, surely he will be caught? He couldn't have gone far, it has only been a few hours, and the girl wouldn't have gone willingly. She will be wanting her parents. We do not know all of the details yet; perhaps Mr Russell has a clue already and they have found her. I'm sure it will all turn out all right. But it's despicable. Kidnapping a child, especially one he abandoned previously."

"I know, that is the worst of it. He thinks nothing of her. He didn't care before whether she lived or died. I fear for her. I fear he will kill her anyway."

"He won't because he wants your money. He won't be stupid enough to hurt her for that reason alone," Philip said.

"What is keeping Mr Russell from being here?"

"I'm sure he will be here soon."

"He had better be!"

"You look well-dressed, even for you. Wasn't it that wedding today?" he asked, trying to diffuse his cousin's anguish.

"Yes. I had to leave early."

"Was it a good wedding?"

"Yes. They were a very happy couple; the bride was radiant. I had to leave after only two dances."

"Well come, come. Sit down. I'm sure all will be well in the end."

"I will stay by the window and watch for Mr Russell," she sighed and she placed herself in the window seat.

The long sought-after person arrived half an hour later and was greeted by his client with clear anxiety.

"Mr Russell, what has kept you? Where have you been?"

"I'm sorry for my delay in getting here," he said. "I have been instructing my staff in their work to recover the child. If I could have got here sooner I would have done." He took off his coat and hat.

"Tell me everything that happened," she said, seating herself.

Mr Russell stood and explained. "I received a letter from Mr and Mrs Prentice two days ago, stating that although their daughter was well, they had been told by one of the servants that a stranger in the village was asking questions about them. They were worried, and therefore told me of the situation. I instructed my man Peterson to go and see them. He travelled to their house this morning, but by the time he got there she had already gone. She was taken in the middle of the night, and nobody knew she was gone until the morning. The ransom note was left on her empty bed."

Louise gasped.

"Do you have the ransom note?" she asked.

"Yes, here. Take a look."

She read it and immediately recognised Risinger's handwriting. It was short and to the point, stating as Mr Russell said in his letter.

"The question is, do we tell the authorities, or not?" Lord Philip asked.

"Absolutely not," Louise said firmly. "I will not risk the child."

Mr Russell responded with a curt nod. "As you wish, Miss Thomas. I thought that would be how you would want to proceed. Of course I have many men looking for her."

"But how did he find out where the child was?" she asked anxiously.

"I wish I knew. Only you and I knew the exact location.

Then of course yesterday I had to tell Peterson, but I only told him the exact address before he left."

"Then it must have been someone in your employ, Mr Russell," Louise said. "Several people in the office must have seen the postmark from Mr Prentice's correspondence. They only ever wrote to you, never to me directly. That was the arrangement. I can only suppose that one of them passed the information on, and it would take Mr Risinger only a little further investigation to establish that a new family had moved into the area with a little girl . . . " her voice trailed off as she struggled with her anguish.

"Miss Thomas, I assure you, my staff are the most trustworthy there are." Mr Russell looked unperturbed at her outburst.

"Well somehow he found out, and you must investigate. Someone who works for you has passed on the information."

Mr Russell said nothing more. He knew Miss Thomas well enough to know that there was no arguing with her now, so he bowed his head and mumbled something about questioning his staff.

She remembered fleetingly that she herself had told only one other person where the child was, all those months ago in her study. Mr Lucas. But no, she was sure she could trust him. He had no reason at all to help Mr Risinger. She trusted him with her secret about Robert Adams – was that not proof of his honesty? He was the very last person she would suspect.

Mr Russell stayed for another hour, answering questions from both Louise and Lord Philip. But eventually they allowed him to take his leave, after he promised to send news of his progress twice every day. The ransom note indicated that the money was to be placed into a Swiss bank account within seven days. She would need only three to gather the funds, but she decided to wait for a few days. She had to hope against hope that the child would be found before then.

After Miss Thomas departed from the wedding reception, Charles fulfilled his promise to her and spoke to Jane a few minutes later. He told her that urgent business had called her away, but no more than that. He couldn't mention the child the real reason for her early departure, but he assured Jane that she was well.

It was a small lie, spoken to avoid compromising his sister's happiness, on this her most special of days. Jane was of course disappointed, but she knew her friend well enough now to know that she wouldn't have left unnecessarily. She couldn't help commenting to her brother, "I saw you two dancing not long ago. I hope you didn't offend her in some way again and chase her away."

"Of course not," he exclaimed, somewhat horrified. "I would never offend her again."

Jane smiled. "Good. Though I will check with Louise when I see her next."

"Do as you wish," he replied gravely.

The wedding party continued for some hours, and Charles, despite his current anguish, fulfilled his role as stand-in father of the bride to the very end.

But in his mind, he resolved he must leave that night and travel to Nottinghamshire and find out for himself what had happened. Mr Russell was commissioned to investigate, but he couldn't stay in London and do nothing. And then what? He didn't know, but he knew he must be armed. There was a pistol stored in the cabinet at home. He would take that.

As soon as the details were planned in his mind, his

thoughts dwelt on the time he had recently spent with Miss Thomas. He looked for the smallest indication that she might still care for him in the same way she had professed before. She had been indifferent to him earlier in the day and it was only when they danced that he felt he was making progress. He would have melted her cool exterior eventually, he was sure. He danced once more that evening, with Jane. If he hadn't been obliged to do so, he wouldn't have bothered. It wasn't that he didn't want to but his mind was in Nottingham.

The wedding had been a bright ray of sunshine to his family after months of dark despair. The loss of their mother affected them all. He had grieved at his father's death all those years ago, but losing his remaining parent was a heavy blow. And yet, through all his sadness what had been the one thing carrying him forward? Even though she told him her affections were at an end, still he couldn't but hope against hope that there remained a glowing ember of love that could be set ablaze again, given time. Because he burned with love for her; his heart quickened at the mere thought of her.

And then he remembered that he had squandered the chance to have her as his own, that he had injured her, been less than a gentleman to her. Worse, he chastened her, insulted her, put her down to a degree for which he hated himself more than he hated anyone before. He burned now, but with the deepest shame at what he had done.

Beautiful, perfect Louise. His Louise. Yes, she would always be his. She had borne everything he wrongly threw at her and she could have ruined him and removed all funding but she chose not to. She bore no malice. The look on her face that day when he threw aside her declaration of love. The tears he caused, the anguish; all his own fault.

Well, he was paying for it now. And it was sweet punishment. He deserved it and he accepted it.

Every time his mind wandered to her, it was quickly chastened by the echo of the words he had used that day: 'more male than female'. Yet he couldn't push her out of his mind, however much the thought of her tormented him. He must help her now, do anything he could to alleviate her current suffering.

Then today, he had made her cry yet again by his stupid thoughtless comment as they waited for the carriage. He sighed and made his way through the crowd and tried to look happy and at ease for Jane's sake, although his heart was anything but.

. . .

It was now four days since Miss Thomas had been given the news of the missing child. She hardly ate, and was pale and drawn as she sat in her drawing room alone for yet another day. The deadline for the ransom fast approached, and she dared not think what Risinger would do to the child if she didn't pay. She must pay. It was a large sum, but what value could be put on a child's life? It would mean she would have to stop any further investments for a few years, but it was a small price.

Mr Russell kept his promise and kept her informed of any progress on the investigation, not that there was anything to report. Mr Risinger was as elusive now as he had been for the many months since his disappearance. She felt helpless, despondent and angry, and cursed herself for not having punished Mr Risinger as he deserved the first time he tried to swindle her.

She went to bed at her usual time, but like the last few nights, sleep eluded her for many hours until sheer exhaustion took over and she finally drifted into a light slumber. At four o'clock she was woken by her maid. She held a letter that had just arrived, and which she passed to her mistresses.

The handwriting she vaguely recognised, but couldn't identify it immediately. She tore it open, desperate for news.

Miss Thomas,

Forgive the late hour of this letter, and the liberty I take. But would you be so kind as to come to my house immediately? I have information on the whereabouts of the missing child. Please keep the reason for your visit a secret, even from your most trust-worthy servants. Although I fear they may know the reason for this unusually timed visit, please conceal everything you can.

Yours,

Charles Lucas

She told the maid to order a cab, then dressed herself quickly. A cab was called, which she took with a footman but whispered the address of the destination to the cab driver so he couldn't hear.

Shortly before five, the cab drew up outside Mr Lucas's house. She alighted silently and knocked on the door, her heart pounding. After what seemed an eternity, the door opened and she walked in.

20

Charles waited by the window in his small drawing room for a sign of Miss Thomas. His ears caught the distant rumble of a carriage and he knew it was her.

It pulled up and a few moments later a dark figure alighted. She wore a black hooded overcloak, but the faint outline of her face confirmed her identity. He would know her anywhere. He heard the knock at the door and the servant let her in, as instructed. Then, a few moments later, the drawing room door opened and she walked in.

"Thank you for coming Miss Thomas." He took her outstretched hand in his for a moment.

"Mr Lucas. Your note was most unexpected, but you have news of the child?"

"Yes, but first, are you sure you were not followed? You told no one you were here?"

"I told nobody. Only the cab driver and my trusted footman I brought with me know I'm here." He noticed a vulnerability in her eyes as she spoke.

"I can assure you, I mean you no harm. Would you be so

kind as to come with me?"

He led her through to the sitting room, a place she knew well through her previous visits to Jane. The house was deathly quiet; only the sound of their footsteps could be heard.

He stood aside once they were inside. The room was dimly lit, with a few candles. Huddled by the fire were Mr and Mrs Prentice and their daughter, the missing child.

It took Louise a few moments to believe what she saw. She looked at Mr Lucas, then at the family again. "Marie?"

"Aunt Louise!" The little girl ran and hugged her. Her arms flew around the child. "Oh Marie! You're safe, you're safe!" Tears sprang into Louise's eyes, and she knelt down and kissed the cheeks of the small dark haired girl she though she were her own flesh and blood.

Then sudden realisation followed, and she grabbed the girl by the shoulders and demanded, "Did he harm you?"

They were interrupted by Mr Lucas saying in a serious, urgent manner, "Miss Thomas, we must act quickly. There is no time to lose."

"Tell me everything you need to." She looked up at his anxious face.

"I have barely time to explain. I will tell you every detail shortly, but I believe there has been a conspiracy to defraud you, although I do not yet know the full extent of the deception. Please believe me when I say that you cannot trust anyone at the moment, not even your servants or friends. I can only hope you will make me the exception."

He continued, "I believe it would be most advisable for the police and the local magistrate to be called immediately. Then, if you would allow me, I would like my brother, Edward to be called. We will need a lawyer."

She hesitated for a moment, then remembered that,

with the child safe, there was no reason why the authorities couldn't be called.

"Very well."

"Thank you. I will be back in a moment, and then I will tell you everything."

He walked out of the room, pulling the door shut as he left.

Louise continued in her earlier burst of emotion. "Oh Marie, I thought I'd never see you again." she said and kissed her face again. She turned to the child's parents, who were in a similar state to Mr Lucas, travel-worn and weary.

"Miss Thomas," Mr Prentice said. "Be assured, Marie has not been harmed. In fact, you will be amazed at what happened."

Mr Lucas returned a few minutes later. "I have done as I said, I'm sure Edward will be here soon. As for the police, I hope they will come presently. Time is of the essence."

Louise was now seated on one of the sofas, next to Marie, who looked as though she were about to fall asleep. Mr Lucas sat opposite her.

"I will tell you everything now," he said.

"Please do," she responded. "I would dearly love to know it all."

He sat back in the chair, and after a moment's pause tried to work out where to begin. "I left for Nottingham the night of Jane's wedding. Using the information that you gave me before you left, I intended to find my way to the house where the Prentices were living." He didn't attempt to explain why he went. But he knew his forthcoming words would shock and distress her and the last thing he wanted to do was to cause his Louise any further pain. He paused momentarily, as if reluctant to disclose what he was about to say.

"When I reached Woodborough village the following morning, it took some time to find out where the family was. The landlord of the inn is a man we're both indebted to. He took a bribe easily and told me. When I reached their cottage, only one servant remained, the housemaid. She was somewhat surprised to see anyone call for the family and said that they had left for a month's trip to Scotland to see relatives. She clearly had no idea that the family were in hiding, but after further questioning I established that they had travelled together and that Marie hadn't been kidnapped. The maid stated that they had been gone above a week, and laughed at me when I asked if the child had been taken by force. She had seen the family leave together."

He rubbed his eyes a little, trying to banish the tiredness, and continued, "Eventually, she gave me the name of the place where they were staying – it was in Edinburgh."

I travelled there as fast as I could, but arrived in Edinburgh too late to do anything that day. The following morning, I managed to locate the Prentices."

Here Mr Prentice, who had sat in silence until now, interjected. "We stayed with my cousin at Mr Russell's advice. He told us to remove ourselves there. He said they feared it was because Risinger had wind of where we were."

"Mr Russell?"

"Yes."

"When did he write?"

"Almost two weeks ago."

Miss Thomas gasped. "Mr Russell has been party to this deception," she whispered, her eyes darting to Charles for confirmation.

"I believe so," he said in a grave tone.

Her head swam. "But he has been my family's lawyer for over forty years," she managed to say.

"That does not exonerate him from any illicit activity."

The truth in his statement hit her, and all at once the betrayal struck her with such force that she covered her face with her hands and cried, "How can I ever trust anyone again? How? It is too much!"

Charles walked over to Louise, and placed a hand on her shoulder, "You can trust me."

She looked up at him. His gentle touch burnt her skin and she never wanted him to take his hand away. "Yes, you're right. I'm sorry."

"It's no matter. Your reaction is completely understandable," replied Charles tenderly, and seeing the tears in her eyes, said, "You have done nothing to provoke this man, yet it seems at every turn he wants to hurt you and turn people against you. He tried to do it to me, but he only succeeded in making me your closest ally." She closed her eyes briefly in acknowledgment and he said in a soft tone, "Please try not to distress yourself." He took his hand away and she felt the loss of his comforting touch.

After Mr Lucas had explained all that happened in the last few days, it was only a short time later that the authorities arrived. It was agreed by all those present that Mr Russell should be arrested and questioned. They acted quickly and left. Louise hoped they were up to the job.

Charles persuaded Louise to allow the Prentices to stay as his guests, until such a time as it was deemed safe for them to return home. She was easily convinced. She didn't want to risk taking them to her house.

Edward Lucas arrived a short time later, and was told of the current situation. He listened attentively, was professional in his advice and assented at Miss Thomas's heartfelt request to take over immediately as her lawyer until the situation with Mr Russell could be resolved.

As the authorities and newly appointed lawyer undertook their commissions, the child was sent to bed and the parents retired for much needed sleep, even though it was the early morning.

"I will return home," Louise said. "Your brother will keep me informed of any important developments."

"But surely you should not return home yet?" Charles said desperately. "Not until Mr Risinger has been captured? Not until we know all who were involved."

"I cannot stay here. If I send for clothes then word will soon get around my staff where I am. Besides, I shall call for the protection of my cousin, Lord Philip."

Charles struggled to contain his sudden jealousy. "Miss Thomas, I do not believe you should contact any friends or family until Mr Russell has been questioned, and if at all possible until Mr Risinger is recaptured."

"But Philip cannot be involved. I know him. He is practically the only family I have. He is as honest as they come. He is a little frivolous in a few of his pursuits, but he would never be party to such a thing."

"I understand all this, but you must let things take their course."

"Philip would have nothing to gain by being involved. Nothing. Twenty thousand pounds is nothing to a man such as he. Why, it's pin money!" Her voice became nearly frantic as she spoke. She knew her cousin would have nothing to do with such a loathsome scheme.

"I know you would like your cousin to help you, but I still believe you should not contact him until Mr Russell has been questioned. Is not the child's long term safety paramount?"

She could offer no further argument and turned away. He had annoyed her, especially because he had shown in the past little enough aptitude when it came to judging good characters from bad.

Eventually, she turned back and managed to say, "Very well, I will stay here for a little longer – at least a few more hours, but only with the understanding that you do not inconvenience yourself. You need sleep."

"Very well. I will sleep here."

He made himself comfortable on one of the sofas, but sleep was far from his thoughts at first and Louise still had many questions unanswered.

The tension between them seemed to ease.

"You haven't told me what happened once you found the Prentices," she remarked.

"I spoke to Mr and Mrs Prentice. They had no idea that you were told the child was kidnapped. They believed all was well. We quickly agreed it would be best if we all travelled back to London together, and then to send word to you once we arrived. We travelled by train, and arrived about an hour before you came here this morning."

She stood up and looked out of the window at the street, which had started to fill with people going about their morning business. She was desperate to overcome the dreadful feeling of betrayal from one of those she had trusted all her life. Such secrets Mr Russell knew, so much harm he could do her! She dreaded to think what he might have already told Risinger, what he might have done already to cause her further injury. She would have to form a contingency plan.

After minutes of reflection like this, she turned around and saw that Mr Lucas had fallen asleep. She smiled at the almost boyish peacefulness of his face. After several minutes, she tore her gaze away. She couldn't sleep herself, but quietly paced the room, unable to resist watching him occasionally, and trying to understand her own feelings towards him. Her heart questioned why he acted on her behalf, going even so far as Scotland to recover the child. Could he love her? Could he have done it for her? No. She called herself a fool for thinking such a thing. He obviously felt obliged to her because of Robert Adams. That was all it was. She silently forgave him his earlier transgression against Philip. She could never be angry with him for long.

A few hours later came the news that Mr Russell had been taken into custody and questioned. It took little persuasion for him to confess everything. Having been so easily discovered, he protested to the police that he had been coerced into it by Mr Risinger. He claimed the whole business had been the other man's idea and he only went along with it because he had some excessively pressing gambling debts.

He readily gave the whereabouts of Mr Risinger in exchange for leniency. Risinger was captured by the afternoon, and in the evening Louise summoned Lord Philip. He came immediately and cancelled a night at a concert in order to talk over the events of the day. Louise was exhausted, but in need of further companionship before she could be persuaded to retire for the evening.

They sat for some time in the sitting room. She was apologetic for her selfishness that kept him away from an evening's entertainment.

"It's nothing. It's only a concert. There will be others," he said. "Did we not a long time ago agree to help each other when we could? If we cannot turn to each other, then I do not know what we will do!"

He took her hand and placed his arm around her to reaffirm their friendship.

Just at that moment the sitting room door opened and Mr Lucas was shown in.

She stood immediately and greeted him. His demeanour tensed when he saw Philip.

"Mr Lucas, do you bring further news of today?"

"Yes, I wanted you to hear it from a friend." He sat down in the chair she indicated. "You know Lord Philip?"

The two men nodded at each other.

"Edward, as you know," Charles said, "has spent the day investigating Mr Russell, and he has uncovered evidence that Mr Russell has been stealing money from you for years."

"Nothing surprises me now," she sighed.

"Is it much?" Lord Philip asked.

"He thinks it may be in excess of twenty thousand pounds, all in all. Mostly from investments."

"Oh," was all she could respond with.

"I'm sorry to be the one to tell you of this. Edward doesn't know yet whether the money may be recovered, but by his own admission, Mr Russell is a gambling man, so he does not hold much hope."

"Thank you Mr Lucas. It was kind of you to bring this news yourself."

"I'm sorry to be the bearer of such bad news. Edward wanted to come himself, but I volunteered my services." He then turned to Lord Philip. "I must apologise to you, too. Earlier today I persuaded Miss Thomas to refrain from contacting you until all the perpetrators were uncovered. I didn't mean any offence to you and I beg your pardon."

"Oh pish, do not worry." Lord Philip waved his hand about. "Louise has told me everything, including that. There is little she ever keeps from me," he said, with a sideways glance at her. "I can't say I wouldn't have done the same myself."

"I would think that Mr and Mrs Prentice will return to Devon shortly," said Charles. "But they are more than welcome to stay at my house for as long as they need. I have told them."

"Thank you. I'm sure they will return to Devon presently. They have been absent from their home for long enough. We may well travel together. I have grown to dislike London a great deal recently. I think I will need time away to recover." She spoke quietly and with such a note of sadness that Charles was overwhelmed by the anguish in her face. But it seemed he was powerless to help her. He wanted to hold her. Comfort her. Kiss her.

"Come now, dear Louise," Lord Philip interjected and stood to place a supportive arm around her shoulder. "Do not grow despondent. I cannot bear to see you thus. You will rally! You need not attend the trial; in fact, it will probably be better that you do not. I will attend for you and tell you everything necessary."

She offered him a small smile. "Before you leave, Mr Lucas, I wanted to thank you for everything you have done. I do not believe I have done it until now. Can you forgive me for such an omission?"

"Yes, but it's not necessary to thank me."

"It is," she said incredulously. "If you hadn't pursued this, and gone to so much trouble, they both would have got away with this scheme."

"Then I accept your gratitude," he said in a stiff manner and without meeting her gaze, for he could bear no further evidence of her tender feelings towards another man.

She noticed his cold manner and couldn't understand

how he could take offence at her words. She could see that his mood had suddenly changed, and he was no longer the open and engaging Mr Lucas who, only that morning, had taken command of a truly desperate situation. But she responded with heartfelt gratitude. "Please, I wouldn't want you to have financial loss for everything you did. Be so kind as to forward all your expenses to me."

That made him look at her with something like anger. "I assure you there was little expense and, even if there were, I wouldn't dream of expecting you to pay me back."

"Leave him be Louise," Lord Philip said. "A gentleman does not ask for such recompense, especially when the recipient is a lady."

She was too tired to argue and she simply nodded. Charles stood up and took his leave.

He stole one last lingering look at her as he left.

As he made his way home, he berated himself. He didn't mean to be so cold, so distant. Sheer exhaustion despite his earlier slumber had caused his emotions to be heightened. But how could he help himself? Not once, but twice he was witness to their obvious intimacy. She had made no attempt to withdraw her hand from Lord Philip's when he entered. And then, later, Lord Philip placed his arm around her shoulder. Cousins did marry; it wasn't unusual, especially with the upper classes.

Such a display would only be shown if they had a special understanding. And then, she had been most fervent in her defence of her cousin earlier that day. No, he must face the fact that the love she had at one time so determinedly given to him had transferred to another. There could be no other reason.

He walked home in a daze; needing sleep, but dreading being kept awake all night by this heartbreaking revelation.

21

Two days later, Mr Russell and William Risinger appeared before the Magistrate's Court under charges of deception and fraud. Further charges of theft were brought against Mr Russell. Bail wasn't applied for, and they were remanded in custody pending their trial.

Word spread quickly around London society about their crimes, particularly Mr Russell's, and there was a small article in The Times related to the charges and who the gentlemen were. Edward Lucas had been efficient at keeping the exact details quiet, but there was still a large amount of speculation as to who Mr Russell had stolen from, and of course, all of his clients were eager to know if they had fallen victim.

Louise kept in constant contact with Edward, and appointed him as her new lawyer permanently. He showed little reaction when she told him her pseudonym Robert Adams, but he was secretly pleased that his brother had benefited from such an eminent lady.

He was, however, somewhat distressed when Miss Thomas insisted that she have a private interview with Mr

Risinger the day of the Magistrate's hearing. He soon found out that when she had set her mind on something, argument was fruitless. He therefore somewhat reluctantly arranged for this unusual meeting to take place.

She sat in the public gallery to watch the proceedings with Lord Philip. Afterwards, as she made her way to the holding area underneath the court, she became agitated. The walls and floor grew more worn as they approached and the musty smell and stench of sewage lingered in the air, adding to her distress.

"Are you sure you do not want me to accompany you?" Lord Philip asked as she gripped his arm.

"No. This is something I must do by myself," she insisted, as they stood outside the cell.

The guard opened the door and she was ushered in. It took her eyes a few moments to adjust to the darkness; there was only one small dirty window the size of a letterbox.

The door closed, and two prison guards stood behind Mr Risinger. He was seated on a wooden chair in shabby prison clothes; his hair was longer and more unkempt than she had ever seen it, and despite his desperate situation, he appeared calm and composed.

"Come to take one last look?" he said in an indignant tone. "You could never resist me, could you Louise? Admit it!"

She said nothing. What could she say in return?

His flicked his head in the direction of the guards. "Why don't you ask them to leave, then we'll see how brave you really are."

She raised her eyebrows. "I'm not as stupid as I used to be. You would like that, wouldn't you? To be alone in a room with me. What would you do? Place your hands around my neck and squeeze as hard as you could?"

"I wouldn't know whether to squeeze your neck or kiss it. Don't go putting ideas in my head now," he retorted.

She shivered at the thought of him kissing her. "I wouldn't dream of it. You're evil enough without the need for help."

"I could have been much more amicable if you had married me."

She gave a small snort. "I never looked at you in that way."

"Pity. I could have been something if I had your money."

"You could have been something without my money – you chose the wrong path."

He responded with a shrug. She wanted this over with quickly, so said with passion in her voice. "Why didn't you go to America?"

"Because I wanted to bring you down."

"And ruin your own life in the process?"

"But what was there for me in America? Why, you only gave me fifty pounds. I would have starved on the street with that measly amount. You were always so generous before. I was almost insulted."

"Perhaps if you had starved it would have saved everyone a lot of trouble and heartache, including Mr Russell. I gave you five thousand pounds before. What did you do with it?"

He didn't respond at first, only looked at her standing before him so defiantly. Finally he said, "When I came back from France I watched you for a while. I wanted one last chance to get money out of you. Imagine my mirth when you became friends with Jane Lucas – the sister of my old school friend."

Louise frowned. It had all been orchestrated. Of course it had.

Risinger continued, "I believed I had successfully turned Charles Lucas against you, but it seems he wants to get into your favour again. Beware Louise, he obviously likes you, or rather your money."

"That always was your problem," she said moving closer to him, then finally bending low, she placed her face directly in front of his.

The guards moved forward nervously, but she put her hand up to stop them.

He raised an eyebrow in query and she continued, "You always judge people by your own low standards."

He smiled, "And his brother is your lawyer. Better watch out; they'll take everything from you if you're not careful. I wouldn't want you to make another mistake." His mouth turned up into a sneer.

"The only mistake I ever made was not having you transported the first time around." She stood up, placing as much space between them as possible.

He laughed. "Well, I'll get to Australia now. I hear the weather is much more agreeable than here."

"Oh, they let you outside, do they?" she replied in a light tone.

At her words, his face clouded with fright and uncertainty, giving her a glimpse of the pathetic creature he really was. She decided to bring the interview to an end.

Looking him fearlessly in the eye for the last time, she told him, "May God protect you from others worse than yourself.'

And, with a rustle of satin, she was gone.

. . .

Seven weeks had passed, and Charles searched the newspapers every day to see if the announcement he dreaded the most was inside. He turned, of course, straight to the 'Engagements' section of The Times and looked through for the names of Miss Louise Thomas and Lord Philip Eldon. But days and weeks passed and still nothing.

He returned to work and decided he would dedicate each working day to her alone and concentrate more on those projects in which Robert Adams was an investor. Every detail was checked and checked again. He wouldn't have her lose money even if it was shortly to become the property of another.

One lunch time, as he took a break, he walked out to a nearby park, where he could stop and think away from the four walls in his office. It was a bright day, full of the promise of the season, and it gave him a new optimism. He sat down on the grass and looked around him at the burgeoning trees, and thought back over the last few months. Jane and Boyd had returned from their honeymoon in a buoyant mood and even more in love than when they left. Boyd was to return to the Tamar, taking Jane, and although Charles was getting used to her belonging to another, he felt lonely at times. He missed his sister most in the evenings, when he was too tired to find work a distraction.

As he made his way back to his office half an hour later, he passed a familiar looking young man walking in the opposite direction. He couldn't place him at once, and with a tip of his hat was about to go on, when the young man stopped him.

"Mr Lucas?" he asked. The young man held out his hand. "We met once at dinner in Devon, at Glazebrook, as Miss Thomas's guests." The young man appeared somewhat unnerved by the recollection.

"Yes! Mr Francis, isn't it? I do apologise, I didn't remember your name until now," he shook his hand.

"Do not trouble yourself. I didn't expect such an eminent man as yourself to remember me from so many months ago. You must attend many such events."

The two of them exchanged general conversation, until Mr Francis asked. "Mr Lucas, would you do me the honour of allowing me to introduce you to my wife? We have only been married a month, but I know she would like to meet you. If you remember – you may not – but Lucy, my wife, had returned from a few months in Paris with Miss Thomas, a few days before we dined there."

Charles was about to refuse on the excuse that he had other more pressing work, but his interest was piqued to meet the woman (or, he surmised, probably a girl) who would be chosen to accompany Miss Thomas to Paris. Why not?

"Thank you, the honour would be mine."

The arrangements were made for the following evening, and Mr Lucas arrived at the appointed time. The address he was given was in a respectable part of town, and the lodgings were somewhat old but clean and bright.

He found his hosts more than ready to receive him in a small parlour they shared with the other lodgers. No one else was present, and Mr and Mrs Francis appeared pleased to see him.

Mrs Francis was, as he had thought, very young. She didn't at first appear to be the sort of girl Miss Thomas would particularly single out. However, after a short while, he noticed that she spoke exactly what was on her mind and appeared honest and open. Worthy attributes indeed.

Mr Francis told him he was working in London for a few months, but would be moving back to Manchester shortly, where they would look for a suitable house. In the meantime, Lucy was enjoying London and insisted that her husband take her to concerts, assemblies and other such amusements. Finally, the most obvious subjects of conversation appeared to have been exhausted.

"My husband tells me you met at Glazebrook," Lucy said, after an awkward silence.

"Yes."

"Did he tell you that Miss Thomas is a particular friend of mine? I went to Paris with her for three months last year," she announced proudly.

"So I hear. Did you enjoy your time there?"

"Immensely. I would love to return one day. We stayed in the most luxurious apartment. It belongs to her cousin Lord Philip. Have you been to Paris, Mr Lucas?"

Upon hearing that name, Charles cringed inwardly, but managed to say, "No. I haven't had the pleasure of visiting Paris."

"There is much talk of Miss Thomas marrying Lord Philip Eldon," Mr Francis remarked.

"Why, that will never happen, my dear!" Lucy exclaimed.

"How so, dearest? You cannot know who Miss Thomas shall or shan't marry."

"But I do. Miss Thomas told me so herself not two weeks ago when we visited Devon. She told me that she could only ever marry one man, and that he, alas, does not love her. And I know it's not Lord Philip."

Charles stared at Lucy, unable to think of which question to ask her first.

Luckily her husband continued. "Did she mention who the gentleman was?" he asked.

"No. But it was a little strange what she said. It was the day before we were to leave for London and I said to her, "Louise, if only you could find someone to love as much as I love Mr Francis," and she said, "Oh but I have, I love a man as you love your husband, but alas he does not love me in return." Of course, I enquired who this man was, and how she knew that he does not love her. But she wouldn't say much. All she said was that he told her once that she was furthest in his mind from what constitutes a wife and that he had told her once he considered her conduct more male than female."

Charles instantly recognised his own words, spoken such a long time ago. His heart leapt.

"What a terrible thing to say to poor Miss Thomas," Mr Francis commented.

"Isn't it?" Lucy said. They both looked at Charles, so he could give his opinion.

"Er, yes, a terrible thing to say. Unforgivable in fact."

Charles felt a surge of hope rising within him.

Mrs Francis continued. "Of course, I cannot begin to comprehend what sort of man could say such a thing to Miss Thomas, or how she could still love him after saying that to her! But she was adamant that she still loved him and that she lived in fear of him marrying someone much more worthy than her."

"That is a tragic tale indeed!" cried Mr Francis. "Poor Miss Thomas. She has been so uncommonly kind to us; her wedding gift was most generous. I would hate to think that she wouldn't find her partner in life. I do wonder who this man could be. I would like to give him a piece of my mind!"

"I too," Lucy stated.

After a moment, Mr Francis asked, "Are you sure she wasn't talking about Lord Philip?"

"Oh yes," Lucy said, "She told me that I had never met the gentleman and I have met Lord Philip. Besides, they are good friends. He wouldn't say such a dreadful thing to her."

Mr Lucas could hardly find words as he sat and comprehended what he heard, but he managed to ask, "She said all this two weeks ago?"

"Yes. Well, actually it was probably about two and half weeks ago."

A slow smile spread across his face. She still loved him.

Looking back, Charles couldn't recall much more of the conversation he shared that evening with Mr and Mrs Francis, which was rather unfortunate because he stayed a further forty-five minutes. He seemed to remember them talking about his work, but his replies were vexing and vague, according to his hosts. Though they commented to each other after he left that he was a pleasant man. He shook both Mr Francis's hands in such a grateful way that they were sure he had enjoyed his time with them and that they would see him again soon.

He walked home at double speed, his heart swelling with passionate love as he thought of Louise. He didn't notice the slight drizzle of rain, or the other people on the street. She still loved him! That was all that mattered.

He had to go to her. He would have gone that night if there had been a train to take him.

When he arrived home he sent word to Ashton that he had urgent business that would take him away for a few days. The servants were given instructions to pack clothes for a short trip and he was ready to travel on the first train to leave London for Axminster the next morning.

The journey to Devon the next day was as frustrating as it was slow. There were several delays, though the train departed London on time. All the way, Charles was filled with nervous anticipation. For although he knew his proposal would be accepted (surely he could now be certain of that), he knew she deserved a proper and worthy explanation of his change of heart. When the train pulled in at

Axminster, there was the added frustration of a heavy shower of rain, as well as an hour's wait for a hired carriage. At least, he reflected ruefully, he had plenty of time to compose a suitable address to her.

Finally, at three in the afternoon, he found himself at Glazebrook, his heart pounding as loudly as his knock on the front door.

22

The servant showed Charles straight to a room at the back of the house, a room he recognised as the library. He felt strange being back in her house again, almost at home, but he had no right to be there. Not yet.

"Miss Thomas is expecting you," the servant said, ushering him in.

Expecting him? But how could she know he was coming to see her? He had told no one.

He stood uncertainly inside the elegantly furnished room and wondered where she was. He could see no sign of her. The servant withdrew, closing the door with a loud click. This must have roused her, because he heard movement behind one of the many bookshelves. He followed the noise and there she was, standing on a small stool, reaching up for a book. Her red patterned dress of chiffon made her look like a butterfly. In an instant all his fears magnified.

"Come in my dear," she said in a bright tone and without looking around. "I was trying to find that volume of poetry we spoke about the other day. Ah, here it is. I knew it was here somewhere!" She took a large book off the shelf, stepped off the stool and dusted the cover with her hand, a soft smile on her lips.

Finally she looked up.

"Mr Lucas!"

She moved back in astonishment, unable to comprehend who was before her. Then, after a few seconds, she forcibly composed herself and curtsied. "How do you do?"

"Very well, thank you," he returned her greeting with a stiff bow. How formal they were. How he longed to be more familiar.

"What a surprise! You're the last person I expected to see today."

"I'm sorry to intrude on you without prior notice."

"That is no matter. Would you like to sit down?" she said, indicating the sofa near them.

He turned towards it and they sat awkwardly at opposite ends.

Silence ensued as she waited for him to explain what he wanted from her.

Then, remembering herself and imagining that he was no doubt waiting for her to dispense with the civilities she asked, "How are your family? They are well?"

"Yes, thank you, they are all well." He gave a small nervous laugh.

"Of course, how stupid of me to ask. I have frequent correspondence with your brother and sister. And you. You're well?"

"Yes, thank you."

"I'm glad."

They descended into silence once again. He looked about the room, packed full of volumes.

"Is there something in particular I can do for you, Mr Lucas?"

"Yes!" he said immediately and sat forwards. Yet he didn't speak. His courage, so strong before he was in her presence, now failed him. He stood up and walked about, paused to look at her, then moving to the window, looked out.

"There was rain earlier, it took some time to get a cab here," he said.

"You travelled here from London today, then?"

"Yes." He paused. "Yesterday I saw Mr Francis and had the pleasure of meeting Mrs Francis."

"I'm glad. I only saw them a few weeks ago, but are they well?"

"Yes. Yes they are."

Silence again.

She shifted in her seat. "Mr Lucas, if you have come to give me bad news on behalf of your brother, then pray, please speak it now. Do not keep me in suspense any longer."

He turned around. "I didn't come to give you bad news. Far from it! Is that why you think I'm here?"

"I do not know why you're here. You haven't said. Perhaps you came to speak to Robert Adams? Is more funding needed in Plymouth?"

"No, Louise." He shook his head and walked over to her, surprised but delighted at his own use of her Christian name. He seated himself as near to her as possible. A footstool beside her rudely blocked her from him, but he pushed it aside and knelt in front of her. He gently detached from her hands the book she was still holding and placed it to one side, then took her hands in his.

"I have been trying to think of the words to say to you all

the way here. Yet still I cannot find them." He gave a small laugh. "I'm no poet. I'm an engineer and my only grasp of words is in the field in which I work. I never thought I would wish to possess the ability to speak words that you deserve. Then I could explain in a fitting manner."

"Then speak plainly sir," she whispered breathlessly.

"I love you."

Her eyes widened. "You love me?"

"Yes, I love you with all my heart."

"But I do not understand. How?"

"How?" he gave a small laugh. "How could I not? How could any man who knows you fail to love you?"

"Oh, do not tell me you love me. We both know that nothing could come of it; you couldn't live a life with me. You would waste away here. You're meant for better, higher things. You're a man of the future and I'm stuck in the past, however much I try not to be."

She tore her hands away, stood up and placed herself by the window, exactly where he had stood a few moments before, looking out across the lawn.

"Louise please, do not remember what I said that day. I was the biggest fool in England. I was blind. Blind to the finest woman in the country. If you will not have me, then I will be alone forever, for no woman could ever match you. Did you not know why I went looking for the child? It was for you, not for Marie or her parents or some vain attempt at reparation. I'm selfish to those I care about, I'm loyal only to those I love. And I love you more than I have loved any other person. Hopelessly and desperately."

She said nothing and didn't move. This wasn't the response he was expecting. It was all going wrong. He grew more desperate. Then he suddenly remembered her other objection. "Louise," he pleaded again. "How can you begin to think that marrying you would waste me away? I'm nothing without you. Please –"

At this, she slowly turned around to face him, her face full of the deepest anguish and hope.

He walked over to her and said nervously, "I know you still love me. What should hinder two people who love each other as we do?"

"Is my love for you that obvious?" She spoke in a lowered, ashamed tone.

"No," he said smiling into her face. "You hid it well, too well. But I shall tell you how I know you love me still, if you promise to marry me."

"I do not care how you know, but I shall accept all the same if you think you could stand to share your life with me."

She flew into his arms, and they held each other for some moments, until he pulled her away just enough so that he could gently kiss her. She yielded readily.

The next few minutes of tender words and kisses were interrupted only by the arrival of Louise's previously expected guest. Mrs Rothers was kindly asked and graciously agreed to postpone their poetry discussion in the light of an unexpected matter of business that had arisen. After dispatching her safely home in one of the Glazebrook carriages, Louise quickly returned to the library to find Charles.

"I almost forgot. I have an engagement ring for you." He took her hand and placed a simple gold band inset with a diamond and two rubies on her finger.

"It's beautiful."

"No," he shook his head. "It's not nearly fine enough for you. But it was my mother's. She bequeathed it to me in the hope that one day I would turn my mind to marriage. I believe she would be very happy you are the one to own it. According to Jane, she greatly favoured a match between us." He bent his head and gave the ring a lingering kiss.

"Yes, I believe she did. I'm now interested to know how you learned I still loved you and how you were so sure of my response to your proposal that you brought a ring with you! Tell me how you knew, if I hid it so well."

"But I gave you a clue earlier," he said.

She thought for a moment, but nothing was forthcoming. Finally he said, "It was Mrs Francis."

"Lucy? What is she to do with it?"

After he related all the conversation from the day before, she retorted, "Then I owe much to dear Lucy and her imprudence in recounting a private conversation. I shall not trust her in the future."

"Don't be angry at her. She was a little thoughtless, but I shall forever be grateful to her for it."

"I hate to think how my happiness depends on her thoughtlessness, as well as the luck which placed Mr Francis in that London street at the same time as you."

"I believe, given time, we would have come to an understanding eventually. I love you too much, and especially after I watched most attentively for the announcement in The Times of your engagement to Lord Philip."

"Most attentively?"

"Yes. I feared, dreaded reading it. It was torture, but I had every reason to believe you would marry him."

"No!" she cried. "Lucy recounted my words well, but how could you possibly think I felt anything other than friendship towards Philip? Besides, he is my cousin!"

"He was always with you. You always sought his companionship and support. He is your cousin; he is respected and wealthy. There are so many reasons why it would make a good match."

"But he is my friend as well as my cousin. I trust him and love him as family, nothing else. There are a hundred men I would marry before Philip. He would make an abominable husband. For me, anyway."

"I don't understand, what about the last time I saw you in London? I entered your home and saw you holding hands and later he put his arm around you. I couldn't bear to see it."

"You were jealous? Was that why you were so cold and distant that day?"

"Yes," he acknowledged.

"I'm all amazement. I hadn't the smallest idea you were jealous." She studied his face. "How could I love Philip when you're in the world?"

"I can hardly believe how well you treated me after how badly I treated you."

"Because you didn't love me back, didn't mean I would stop loving you, or wish you ill. In fact, it was the opposite. I knew I wasn't good enough for you."

"Don't say that! Never say that again. It's I who am not worthy of you, all goodness that you are."

"But how did you start to love me? Though it pains me to remember, you hated me so much before."

"It happened gradually. I didn't realise my feelings were love at first. Then when Risinger interfered . . . " he sighed. "I believe I knew I loved you when I saw your workroom that day in the rain. I knew I had misjudged you in every way, not only in believing the wicked words spoken against you. It grew from there very quickly."

"I destroyed the workroom. The day after you all dined

here I couldn't bear the shame of my inadequate education. I was embarrassed. I still am, in a way." She bowed her head.

"Embarrassed? Why?"

"I have tried to dismiss Mr Boyd's words, but they were spoken so honestly. He truly believed that it was a child's room. I couldn't bear it."

She fought back tears.

"But why be embarrassed about an honest interest, and the wish to further your education? Did you destroy everything?"

"Yes. No. I mean, I burnt all the journals and broke many other things. I didn't go in there for a long time, but eventually I cleared it up. I still use it now, though I have not read the journal for a long time. That is why I had not read your bridge article."

He touched her face and murmured, "Oh Louise," then recollecting something else, he said, "Did the equipment and books I sent help?"

"You sent them?"

"Yes."

"I thought they were from Mr Boyd. For a fleeting moment I thought they may have been from you, but I believed he sent them as an apology."

Many further hours that day were spent in similar discussion. They quickly established that they both wished to marry without delay. Too much time had been wasted already. In the early evening they walked out and she showed him the lake, the fields beyond the gardens and the beautiful scenery she so loved. He showed little interest in anything other than his companion.

As they walked back to the house, he commented, "You are quiet."

"I was trying to remember the last time I was this happy," she said.

"When was that?"

"I have never been this happy," she replied.

Charles stayed a week in Devon. His strict sensibilities wouldn't allow him to stay as a guest in her house without a chaperone, so he put up at the local inn.

As word spread of the engagement, the landlord transferred Mr Lucas to his best room. Custom increased; everyone it seemed wanted to see first hand what sort of man the future master of Glazebrook was and possibly catch a glimpse of him. Many were disappointed, because he spent most of his time at his future home.

Louise travelled back to London with him, under the excuse that she needed to visit her dressmaker for her wedding gown. Although their courtship in London was short, every day was delightful. She especially enjoyed his attentions at evening engagements, when he would approach her as soon as she arrived and tenderly kiss her hand. He would stay determinedly at her side, except when an unkind friend parted them, and he would always see her safely home afterwards.

Jane was ecstatic when she learnt of the news. She couldn't have wished for a better sister, but when she next met her brother, she chastened him for keeping his feelings towards Louise such a secret.

"If I had known of your love, I could have helped you both on the way to happiness," she said.

"That is what I was afraid of," he replied.

The wedding was the occasion of the year. They married in the chapel at Glazebrook and Louise was declared a vision in her cream silk gown and lace trim. "Never was there a more beautiful bride," Lord Philip said, as he waited to escort her to the chapel. "If I could find a woman with half your sense then perhaps I could one day be persuaded into matrimony."

Louise laughed at him. "I still believe you will fall in love with someone who will not return your sentiments."

Rather than be fashionably late arriving at the chapel, Louise was a few minutes early. She could not wait a moment longer to be married to her beloved Charles. She anxiously looked to the front of the church to find her nervous, fiancé smiling back at her.

After the ceremony, Louise placed her bouquet on her father's grave. "See, I chose wisely, father," she whispered.

Six months into the marriage, the dependents at Glazebrook were satisfied that nothing had really changed. The head cook was a little happier, since Charles's presence each night at dinner meant that her mistress was always wanting to vary her menu.

At first, Charles was a little overwhelmed by the constant visitors wishing the newly married couple well. As time went on, however, his wife would make excuses for him being absent at such visits due to his engineering commitments, which he pursued whenever possible in her restored workroom.

Jane and her husband were frequent visitors, and eventually so were Edward and his wife. Charles watched Louise revel in the novelty of family life, truly enjoying every moment with her brother and sister, nieces and nephews, who in the fullness of time became close companions to their own children, the heirs to Glazebrook.

And, as well as offering gardens and fields aplenty for family gatherings, the estate and house were large enough to provide times of peace and solitude, especially for a man and a woman who had found a deep and binding love against the odds.

The End

DEAR READER, if you enjoyed this novel, I would really appreciate it if you would leave a review. It really helps other people find my books.

Read the second book in this duet series Hidden Hearts: *The Tutor's Secret, A Historical Victorian Clean Romance:*

"In the elegant streets of Bath, Adella's tranquil life as a former governess in Devon is upended when her past resurfaces in the most unexpected way. Five years ago, she was left heartbroken and jilted by Joel, a charming tutor with a mysterious life beyond his lessons. Their romance was a whirlwind of passion and promises until Joel's abrupt departure and devastating betrayal.

Now, Joel returns, not as the tutor she once loved, but under his true identity, revealing a secret so profound it could alter everything Adella believed about their past. As their paths collide in the present, Adella is forced to confront the haunting memories and the staggering truth of Joel's deception. Torn between resentment and a lingering spark of love, she must decide whether to hold onto her grievances or embrace a second chance at love, fully aware of the monumental secret that Joel carries. Can Adella navigate the turbulent waters of love and deceit, or will Joel's hidden past be too great a barrier for their hearts to overcome?"

www.ingramcontent.com/pod-product-compliance
Lightning Source LLC
Chambersburg PA
CBHW061544210726
48287CB00006B/2077